DEER ON THE DRIVE

Michelle took charge. 'Now look at it this way,' she began brightly. 'The best thing we can do for the deer, for Honey-Mum and Sprite, is to make a really good film about them.'

'You mean, show people how interesting they are?' James said thoughtfully.

'And encourage them to come to Glisterdale,' Mandy exclaimed.

'Exactly!' Michelle said, smiling. 'Look at it as a challenge. We've only got a few days to do it. Let's make this the best film we can.'

Mandy nodded. 'Right!' she said, in her most positive voice, 'Come on, James, let's get cracking!'

Animal Ark series

LUCY DANIELS

Deer
— *on the* —
Drive

Illustrations by Ann Baum

*Hodder
Children's
Books*

a division of Hodder Headline Limited

Special thanks to Tanis Jordan
Thanks also to C. J. Hall, B.Vet.Med., M.R.C.V.S., for reviewing
the veterinary information contained in this book.

Animal Ark is a trademark of Working Partners Limited
Text copyright © 1999 Working Partners Limited
Created by Working Partners Limited, London W6 0QT
Original series created by Ben M. Baglio
Illustrations copyright © 1999 Ann Baum

First published in Great Britain in 1999 within *Wildlife Ways*
by Hodder Children's Books

This single volume edition 2000

The right of Lucy Daniels to be identified as the author of this
work has been asserted by her in accordance with the Copyright,
Designs and Patents Act 1988.

10 9 8 7 6 5 4 3 2

A Catalogue record for this book is available from the British Library

ISBN 0 340 73665 8

Typeset by Avon Dataset Ltd, Bidford-on-Avon, Warks

Printed and bound in Great Britain by
Clays Ltd, St Ives plc

Hodder Children's Books
a division of Hodder Headline Limited
338 Euston Road
London NW1 3BH

One

'What do you think, Mum, shorts or trousers?'
Mandy Hope came into the kitchen holding a
pair of brown shorts in one hand and a pair of
khaki trousers in the other. 'I can't decide.'

Emily Hope stopped buttering toast and
turned her head to look.

'Hmm. Difficult,' she answered. 'I know we're
having a hot August, but if you're trekking
through woods up at Glisterdale, you'll need a
bit of protection from thorns and nettles. I'd
go for trousers.' She blew a wayward red curl
off her forehead. 'Ask Dad what he thinks.'

'Ask Dad what he thinks about what?'
Adam Hope said, coming into the kitchen from

the garden, carrying a bowl of freshly-picked loganberries.

'Trousers or shorts?' Mandy held them both up.

'Oh, of course, I'd forgotten, my TV presenter daughter is off on location today,' Mr Hope teased. 'Definitely trousers, more professional. So, Mum and I have got to manage without you again, have we?'

'Da-ad,' Mandy groaned. 'You're just trying to make me feel guilty. You know I've made a deal with Simon while this project is on.' She made a face. 'I promised I'll do all the jobs he wants me to when the filming is finished.'

Mandy's parents were both vets and their practice, Animal Ark, was housed in the modern extension built on to the back of the old stone cottage that was their home. Simon was their practice nurse. Usually Mandy helped out after school and during the holidays but Simon had agreed to do her chores while Mandy and her best friend James Hunter helped Michelle Holmes, the presenter of the TV programme *Wildlife Ways*, to make a film about deer.

'I'm only joking, love. What's the plan for today?' Adam Hope sprinkled a handful of loganberries over his breakfast cereal.

'I'm meeting James outside the post office and Michelle's picking us up there, on her way to Glisterdale,' she looked at her watch, 'in ten minutes' time!'

'Mandy!' called Mrs Hope, as Mandy headed for the door. 'Eat some toast.'

'And that's an order,' laughed her dad. 'Then you'd better scoot, you don't want to keep the others waiting.'

Mandy grabbed a piece of toast, then rushed upstairs to get dressed. With seconds to spare she raced down the lane and across the green, arriving at the post office just as Michelle's Jeep pulled up by the bench where James was already waiting. Janie Doyle, the *Wildlife Ways* camera operator, was in the front seat, polishing a camera lens.

'Hi there, you two,' Janie said, turning round to face Mandy and James as they scrambled into the back of the Jeep. 'Can you fill me in on Glisterdale Grange?' She ran her hand through her short blonde hair. 'Michelle said you released a fawn there once.'

'Yes, we found a fawn in the forest behind the Old School House in Welford,' Mandy began. 'Her mother had died and we needed somewhere safe to release her.'

'Mr Dickenson owns the Grange,' James continued. 'He's got a herd of fallow deer and a tame doe called Honey-Mum. She adopted Sprite.'

'So did you already know Peter Dickenson?' Janie asked.

'No,' Mandy replied. 'We met Mr Dickenson after I found his dog, Rosie, stuck down a rabbit hole. It was just after we found Sprite and we were desperate to find a place to release her that would be safe.'

'That's when Mr Dickenson offered us Glisterdale Grange,' James finished off.

'I must say, Mr Dickenson sounded extremely helpful and friendly on the phone,' Michelle said, looking in the rear view mirror and signalling to turn left. 'He was very keen for us to film his herd.'

'You know, Glisterdale Grange is open to the public. I bet loads of people will visit once they've seen the deer on television,' said Mandy, as they left the main road and drove towards the entrance.

'Sprite might be a star!' James added.

'I really hope we see her today,' Mandy said enthusiastically.

'It would be great for the film to see how the little fawn is getting on,' Michelle grinned. 'And if, as you say, the deer go very near the house, that will make our job much easier.' She turned the Jeep between the big gates and on to the wide gravelled drive that curved in a semicircle around the house. The house was enormous, built of honey-coloured stone that shone in the sunlight. It had a big forecourt with an information office and a place where the public could park. To the side of this was an area with wooden tables and benches for picnics.

Michelle drove around the house, past the office and into a small car park marked: Private – Estate Personnel Only.

'I called in and saw Tony Morris, the estate manager, yesterday and he said we could park here,' she told them, as she turned off the engine. 'He thought that Peter Dickenson might walk around the estate with us and show us the best places to see the deer. We'll just decide where we want to film today, and then start work tomorrow.' Gathering up her notebook, Michelle got out of the Jeep. Like Mandy, she wore khaki trousers and a khaki shirt. She had a brown sweatshirt with *Wildlife Ways* emblazoned across the front slung around her shoulders.

'Mr Dickenson is really friendly,' Mandy told them, as she scrambled out of the Jeep.

'He always gives us an update on Sprite when we visit,' James added, climbing out of the back seat after Mandy.

While Michelle was locking up the Jeep, three men wearing bright yellow hard hats came around to the front of the house.

'There's Mr Dickenson!' Mandy waved at one of the three men and was about to run over to him, but he just smiled at her and then looked away.

'That's Tony Morris with him,' said Michelle. 'They look pretty busy.'

They watched as the third man flicked through pages and pages of notes on a clipboard, and pointed up at the roof. 'I don't think we should interrupt him now,' Michelle decided. Mandy nodded. She could see that Mr Dickenson looked worried.

'Why don't we take a look around the estate on our own?' Janie suggested, gathering up her bag and a light meter. 'We can catch up with them later.'

Mandy and James led Michelle and Janie down towards the paddocks at the far side of the house where a path led into the forest.

'Look!' whispered James. 'Over there!' Stepping slowly along the path were five fallow deer. They watched as the group, three adult females and two fawns, made their way daintily across the paddock, their spotted coats glossy in the sunlight.

Mandy gasped softly. 'Aren't they beautiful!' she breathed.

Suddenly, the doe at the head of the group stopped and jerked her head in their direction. She gave a sharp little bark, stamped her feet and raised her tail to show the white fur underneath, warning the others of danger. All five deer froze.

Then, just as quickly, the deer decided that the humans were not a great threat and continued picking their way across the paddock, nipping at bushes and shrubs as they passed by. Mandy could hear the soft tap of their hooves as they crossed the drive and disappeared back into the forest on the other side of the house.

'They are very trusting,' Michelle observed. 'Most deer would be extremely nervous to be this close to humans. It shows how safe they must feel here.'

'Oh, they are safe,' Mandy said happily. 'Mr

Dickenson wouldn't let *anything* happen to his deer.' She grinned.

Michelle, Janie, Mandy and James spent the next couple of hours walking along the nature trail through the estate. In the forest there were lots of glades and patches of open grassland where deer would gather.

'I'm not surprised the deer are doing well here,' Michelle observed. 'This is exactly the sort of forest that fallow deer love.' She gestured with her arm. 'Lots of shrubs and bramble patches, and long grass, perfect for hiding a newborn fawn. Did you know that when a fawn is born it has no scent at all for twenty-four hours?' She laughed at the surprise on Mandy and James's faces. 'So when the mother leaves it to browse, as long as the fawn keeps perfectly still, it need have no fear of predators.'

'So if you find a newborn fawn you should leave it alone?' Mandy asked.

'That's right.' Michelle nodded emphatically. 'Except of course when, like with Sprite, you know the mother is dead. But under normal circumstances, if you touch it you will give the fawn your smell. That will really upset the mother.' She waited while Janie took a reading from the light meter. 'And if the mother comes back while humans are around, that will frighten her off.'

'So the mother might abandon it, even though you haven't touched the fawn?' James asked.

'It's possible,' Michelle replied. She looked up at the sky and stretched out her hand. 'Uh, oh, I think we're in for some rain.' As they'd been walking, the sky had turned a dark yellowy-grey and now thunder rumbled in the distance.

'I think we'd better make a run for it,' Janie said. 'I don't want to get this light meter wet.'

By the time they made it back to the house, the rain was bucketing down. Mrs Dickenson was waiting with the kitchen door open, holding Rosie, the Dickensons' Lakeland terrier, by the collar. 'Come in, quickly,' she called.

Above the kitchen door a cracked gutter had come adrift and water was pouring straight down the wall. In her excitement at seeing Mandy, Rosie lurched forward. Mandy dodged sideways to avoid stepping on Rosie's paws and was hit by the stream of rainwater.

'Ugh, Rosie! I'm soaked, thanks to you!' Mandy said, picking the little dog up and giving her a hug. Mrs Dickenson passed her a towel and then turned to Michelle. 'You must be Michelle Holmes?' she said.

'That's right,' Michelle smiled. 'And this is Janie Doyle, my camera operator.'

Mandy rubbed at her wet hair. 'We've been looking for places to film, Mrs Dickenson,' she said. 'But we didn't see Sprite or Honey-Mum.'

Mrs Dickenson smiled, but Mandy thought her mind seemed to be on something else. While she was pouring them mugs of steaming tea, she kept glancing at the door that led to the hallway. Suddenly they heard footsteps approaching, and Mrs Dickenson tensed. James shot Mandy a puzzled look and she realised he had noticed that something was wrong too.

'OK, Tony, I'll see you later at the bridge and we'll check on the sheep.' As Peter Dickenson pushed open the kitchen door, his voice sounded weary and dejected. 'Hello, everyone,' he said, ushering another man in and gesturing for him to sit down. James shuffled round the table to make room for Mr Dickenson, who sat down, ran his fingers through his hair and gave a deep sigh. Rosie came trotting over to him and sat quietly at his feet.

Mrs Dickenson passed the two men cups of tea before asking softly, 'Tell me, is it very bad?'

'Yes, I'm afraid it is.' Mr Dickenson smiled grimly at his wife. 'In fact it couldn't be much worse.' He shook his head.

Michelle looked at Mandy and James, who fidgeted uncomfortably. 'This is obviously a bad time, perhaps we should go?' Michelle offered.

Peter Dickenson looked at her. 'My apologies,' he said. 'I'm neglecting you, Michelle. I'm so busy worrying about my troubles that I completely forgot you were coming to see us about the programme. I am sorry.'

'No problem,' Michelle smiled reassuringly. 'We can always come back another time.'

'You can if we're still here!' Mr Dickenson said bluntly.

'Oh, Peter!' Mrs Dickenson hurried over and stood behind him with her hands on his shoulders, looking at the shocked faces of the others.

'What?' Mandy exclaimed. 'Why wouldn't you be here?'

'Perhaps you'd like to explain, Charles,' Peter Dickenson asked the other man.

'Of course. My name is Charles Gregg and I'm a surveyor,' he introduced himself. 'I'll keep it fairly simple. To open a house like this to visitors you need what's called public liability insurance.' He shifted in the chair and shuffled the sheaf of papers in front of him. 'So, the insurance company obviously want to know that the house is safe, that ceilings are not going to fall down on visitors' heads or floors give way. That would cost them a lot of money in claims.' He paused. 'The problem is that this house *isn't* safe,' said Mr Gregg. 'And in a nutshell, without the necessary repairs, the house will have to be closed to the public.'

Mandy gasped. She couldn't believe it.

'What's the actual problem?' asked Michelle, with a frown. 'The house looks pretty sound from outside.'

'That's just it, Michelle,' Peter Dickenson explained. 'You don't always know a problem exists. We tend to live mostly down here in what used to be the old servants' quarters. It's nice and cosy. But the big rooms in the rest of the house, the ones we open to the public, are damp and full of wet and dry rot.'

'What *are* wet and dry rot?' James asked.

'Basically, they are both caused by fungi,' Mr Gregg told them.

'Fungi, like mushrooms?' James said, surprised.

'Yes, that's right.' Mr Gregg explained. 'Both

wet rot and dry rot are caused by a fungus that thrives in damp places. This house has internal gutters that have been slowly leaking. Good York stone, like the stone this house is built of, can absorb a lot of water and still dry out with no harm done. But all the timbers in the west wing are rotten and need to be replaced. The trouble is, dry rot spreads like wildfire.' He shook his head. 'I'm afraid work on the west wing will have to start immediately if the damage isn't to spread to the rest of the house.'

Mrs Dickenson swallowed hard. 'How much is it likely to cost?' she asked.

'It's going to cost a fortune,' Peter Dickenson sighed, looking up at his wife. 'It could be nearly a quarter of a million pounds.'

Mandy and James looked at each other, stunned. No wonder the Dickensons were worried.

'Why do you need to have Glisterdale Grange open to the public?' Mandy asked.

'We depend on the money, Mandy,' Mr Dickenson told her. 'People pay to see the gardens too, but that's only in summer. In order to keep the estate going we need to keep the house open for most of the year.' He put his hands together and leaned his chin on them.

'Nowadays, Mandy, estates and houses like this have to pay for themselves.'

'And anyway,' added Mrs Dickenson, 'we couldn't let this beautiful house simply fall down around our ears. This is our home.'

'Quite right!' Mr Dickenson said in a positive voice. 'We'll have to find a way.'

'Could I make a suggestion?' Charles Gregg asked, taking a plan of the estate out from among his papers. 'You have quite a lot of land here that doesn't produce any income. Have you considered selling any of it?'

'No!' Peter Dickenson was adamant. 'The last thing I'd want to do is break up the estate.'

'Suit yourself,' Mr Gregg said, 'but if you change your mind I happen to know a buyer who would take that woodland there,' he pointed to Glisterdale Forest on the plan he had in front of him, 'off your hands for well above the market price.' He folded the plan and put it away. 'It would be a perfect solution to your problem.'

James was frowning deeply. Mandy guessed he was thinking the same as she was. Surely Mr Dickenson wouldn't sell the deer wood. He couldn't! She thought of Sprite and Honey-Mum, and a lump came into her throat.

'I'm sorry, I just couldn't do it.' Mr Dickenson shook his head. 'I couldn't sell Glisterdale Forest.' Mandy let out a huge sigh of relief as he said, 'We'll just have to find another way round this problem.' He smiled at Mandy and James. 'Now, if you'll excuse me, Charles, these people have a film to make in that very woodland and I've held them up long enough.'

'Don't forget,' Charles Gregg said, as he got up to leave. 'If you change your mind about the woodland, just let me know.'

'I won't.' Mr Dickenson opened the door to see him out. 'I'm sure of that!'

He closed the door behind Mr Gregg and turned back to where Mandy and her friends were sitting at the kitchen table.

'I've seen enough of the woodland to have a good idea of what we want to do,' Michelle said brightly. She looked over at Janie who nodded. 'If it's all right with you, we'll start first thing in the morning?'

'Fine,' Peter Dickenson said, sounding more cheerful. 'The film might help bring more visitors to the grounds of Glisterdale Grange. That will be a help.'

Mandy was thoughtful as they walked back to Michelle's Jeep.

'What's wrong?' James asked quietly.

'It's just that everything seemed so, well,' Mandy hunted for the right word, '*safe* here a little while ago and now it all seems in danger.'

'I know what you mean,' James agreed. 'But Mr Dickenson won't sell the deer wood. You heard him say so.'

Mandy nodded but she was glum and quiet on the way home.

That evening, after Mandy had spilled out her worries about Glisterdale Grange, Adam Hope tried to reassure her. 'Don't get too upset, Mandy. Peter Dickenson loves his land, he won't sell it if he can possibly avoid it,' he told her. 'If there is any way at all of sorting things out, he'll find it.'

Mandy sighed. She knew her dad was right, but what if there *wasn't* any other way to raise the huge amount of money? What would happen to the deer then?

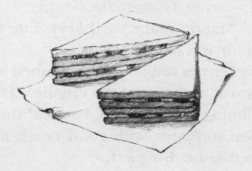

Two

The next morning, as soon as Mandy opened her eyes, she sprang out of bed and leaned out of the window. The sun was shining and the still air was already warm. Everywhere looked fresh and green after yesterday's rain. A perfect day for filming deer, Mandy thought to herself. She dressed quickly and set off to meet the others.

When they arrived at Glisterdale Grange, Peter Dickenson was standing on the drive next to his car. He looked hot and uncomfortable in a dark suit with a green and white striped tie. 'I'm off to see the bank manager,' he announced. 'I thought I'd better dress the part! I only wear this suit on special occasions.'

'Well, saving Glisterdale Grange is pretty special,' Mandy said. 'We'll keep our fingers crossed for you all day.'

Mr Dickenson laughed as he climbed into the driver's seat and started the engine. 'That will make filming a bit difficult, I should think,' he said. 'See you later, with good news, I hope.' He waved as he drove off.

Mandy and James helped Janie to unload her equipment.

'Mandy, could you put this spare cassette of film in that bag in the back of the Jeep, please?' Janie asked, as she slotted a cassette into the camera. 'And could you find a filter in that case for me, please, James?' She nodded her head towards a square aluminium case.

James opened the lid. The case was full of camera equipment. 'That's it, in the flat box,' Janie said, as James picked it out.

'We'll start with the paddock and the gardens,' Michelle said, gesturing towards the paddock where all the new young trees had metal guards around them. 'I want to show how the new trees and the formal gardens are protected from hungry deer.'

They opened the gate and entered the paddock.

'Why do the tree guards have to reach so high?' James asked. 'They must be at least two metres in height and the deer aren't that tall.' He stretched his arm up but couldn't reach the top. Janie began filming with James alongside the trees to show the height of the guards.

'Good question, James,' Michelle said. 'You'd be surprised how high a deer can reach when they stand up on their hind legs. If the guard isn't high enough they can get to the bark and eat it, and that kills the tree.'

'So once the tree has hardened up, they won't be able to harm it?' Mandy asked.

Michelle nodded. 'Deer don't do any damage to the bark of an established tree. But they can strip the bark completely from a young tree or even trample it down. Let's move a bit closer to the gardens.' She led them up on to a wooden bridge, over a ditch, and through the deer-proof gate into the formal gardens. Brilliantly-coloured roses grew beside red and pink geraniums. In the middle of one of the flowerbeds, an old man in green overalls and a straw hat was pruning bushes.

Michelle introduced herself, Mandy and James. Janie turned her camera on again.

'We're here to film the deer,' Mandy told the man.

'An' I'm here to do me job, so I won't stop. Me name's Albert, by the way.' With a series of efficient snips, he cleared a floribunda rose of all its dead blooms. 'But you can call me Bert.'

'Do the deer ever get into the gardens and damage the flowers, Bert?' Michelle asked.

'What!' Bert looked aghast. 'Never!' he declared. 'They'd strip 'em down as fast as you could say Jack Robinson.'

'But how do you keep them out?' James asked, waving away a wasp that was dangerously close to getting behind his glasses. 'There isn't a fence.'

'Don't need no fences, the ha-ha keeps 'em out,' Bert told them, carrying on with his pruning. 'Works a treat.'

'The what?' Mandy said, puzzled. 'What's a ha-ha?'

Bert put down his secateurs. Then he walked over to the bridge and pointed at the ditch, waiting as they gathered around. 'You digs a ha-ha,' he explained, pointing at the ditch, 'all around the gardens. And what you digs out of the ditch you makes into a steep bank. Deer don't get down there.'

'It's like a moat without water,' James exclaimed.

'And it's much better than building a wall,' Michelle said, 'because it doesn't hide the view.'

'Look now, over there,' Bert said, pointing to a patch of shrubs near a copse of trees. As they watched, a herd of about twenty deer pranced out from among the trees into the open and ran fleetly across the grass to the sheep paddock. When they reached the paddock they swerved and changed direction, now running up the hill towards the forest. They stopped in the shade of a massive oak tree.

Through her binoculars Mandy searched for Honey-Mum and Sprite, but the spotted does all looked similar and the fawns were all jumping about, playing together. She could see that some of the deer were black and one was creamy white, but most were spotted, although some had light-coloured coats and others were much darker.

'Do you know if one of those is Honey-Mum?' Mandy asked Bert eagerly. 'We're hoping to film Sprite, the fawn she adopted.'

'The fawn'll be running with the herd now,' Bert told them. 'You'll not pick that fawn out, 'cept if you tagged it.' Bert raised an eyebrow quizzically at Mandy.

Mandy shook her head frowning. 'But I'm sure I would recognise her by her coat,' she said. 'She's a golden chestnutty colour with rows of spots on her back and sides.'

'So she's a common, then,' Bert observed, looking at Michelle who nodded.

'Sprite's a fallow deer,' James said, puzzled. 'Like those ones.' He pointed at the herd.

'Aha!' said Bert wisely. 'All them deer are fallow. Fallow deer come in four types, you see.' He looked from Mandy to James to check that they were paying attention. 'There's *black* 'cause they're black, *menil* – that's pale spots, *white* 'cause they're light with light-coloured hooves instead of black, and *common* 'cause they're . . . well . . .' Bert paused.

'Common?' suggested Mandy, and they all laughed.

'Been fallow deer here for years and years,' Bert told them. 'Lovely creatures. Have to be well managed, though, else they get out of hand.' He turned back to his roses. 'I've got to get on now. If you find your fawn, ask Mr Dickenson about tagging her.' He was interrupted by a wailing cry that sounded like a cat miaowing.

'Whatever's that?' James asked.

'That's a peacock,' Bert chuckled. 'Sounds like a banshee, he does.'

A splendid peacock, followed by several peahens, came strutting from behind a hedge down to the ornamental pond in the middle of the gardens. While the others were drinking, one of the peahens turned and came bounding down, flapping her wings excitedly. She made a beeline for James and lay down in front of him, fixing him with a beady eye.

'She's taken a shine to you, lad,' Bert said, laughing, as James blushed and backed away.

'I wish she would take a shine to someone else!' James muttered, as the peahen tried to follow him.

They had lunch at one of the wooden tables in the picnic area at the side of the house. There were slices of vegetarian quiche, and cheese and tomato sandwiches, but Mandy found that she wasn't hungry. She was too busy thinking about Sprite. 'Why didn't we think to tag her?' she wondered aloud.

'Don't worry too much, Mandy,' Michelle advised. 'After all, you say Mr Dickenson has been giving you progress reports, so he must be able to recognise her.'

'Of course!' exclaimed James. 'Perhaps he can point her out to us.'

'Why don't you ask him,' Michelle laughed. 'Here he comes now.'

They watched as Peter Dickenson got out of his car. He went around to the other side and gathered up his crumpled jacket and sheaf of papers from the passenger seat. Slowly and wearily, he walked towards the little group at the picnic table. Mandy's heart sank. She looked at James and could see that he sensed Mr Dickenson's dejection too. Peter Dickenson stopped to wait for his wife who was hurrying over from the house, Rosie bounding joyfully ahead of her. They exchanged a few words, then joined Mandy and the others at the picnic table.

'I just don't know how to tell you this,' Mr Dickenson sighed, dropping the papers on the table. Mrs Dickenson was looking at him anxiously. 'I have seen *everybody*,' he said forlornly, 'and it's hopeless.' Mandy stared at him in horror. 'Everybody I spoke to said the same thing,' he told them, looking at his wife. 'Sell some land.'

'Oh, Peter, does it have to be that?' Mrs Dickenson's eyes were bright with tears.

'There's no other choice. I've tried everything else.' With a deep sigh he rifled through the papers and pulled out several typed sheets of thick cream paper. 'Charles Gregg kindly worked out the cost of the work for me.' He passed it to his wife.

'But Mr Dickenson,' Mandy asked quietly, biting her lip. 'Which bit of land are you going to sell?'

'Mandy, I'm afraid I don't have a choice. The only land that it's feasible to sell is Glisterdale Forest,' said Peter Dickenson, shaking his head. 'The buyer Charles Gregg knew of is so keen to get it that he's coming over this afternoon to discuss terms.'

'But what about the deer?' Mandy felt herself go cold. 'What about Honey-Mum and Sprite?' she asked.

'Well, I hope that nothing will change too drastically. I've asked that the deer herd be left alone.' Mr Dickenson managed a weak smile. 'I'm sure you can carry on with your film. The possible purchaser is coming over later to have a look so you can ask him then, but I can't imagine he'd raise any objections.'

'Thanks,' Michelle said, standing up. She nodded at Mandy and James. 'Perhaps we'd better get on,' she suggested tactfully. 'I'm sure Mr and Mrs Dickenson have lots to discuss.'

Mandy gathered up the leftovers and put them in the bin. She didn't want to hear any more about the forest being sold. The whole thing was awful. She and James silently followed Michelle and Janie back through the paddocks and into the woods. Noticing how miserable they looked, Michelle took charge. 'Now, look at it this way,' she began brightly. 'The best thing we can do for the deer, for Honey-Mum and Sprite, is to make a really good film about them.'

'You mean, show people how interesting they are?' James said thoughtfully.

'And encourage them to come to Glisterdale,' Mandy exclaimed.

'Exactly!' Michelle said, smiling. 'Look at it as a challenge. We've only got a few days to do it. Let's make this the best film we can.'

Mandy nodded. 'Right!' she said, in her most positive voice, 'Come on, James, let's get cracking!'

'Good,' said Michelle, handing Mandy a microphone to carry. 'Now, let's find ourselves some deer.'

*   *   *

By the end of the afternoon they were all feeling more cheerful. The deer seemed undisturbed by the filming and Janie had got some wonderful close shots of them feeding and plenty of footage of the fawns playing.

'I bet we'll see Sprite soon,' James said, optimistically.

'I'll ask Mr Dickenson about her when we get back,' said Mandy, taking off her trainer to tip out a stone. 'But I'm still sure I'll know her when I see her.'

They were tired as they made their way back to the house, but pleased with the day's work. As they stepped out of the wood and into the sunshine Mandy screwed up her eyes. A Land-rover was parked outside the house, and Mandy recognised the registration number at once.

'Oh no,' she moaned to James. 'What's *he* doing here?'

Michelle shaded her eyes with her hand and stared at the man who was getting out of the passenger's door. 'Isn't that Sam Western?' she asked.

'Too right,' James agreed glumly, 'and Dennis Saville.'

Michelle made a face. 'Let's walk slowly,' she said. 'Then perhaps by the time we reach the house they'll have gone. I have no wish to meet that awful man again.'

Sam Western was a local farmer who had recently tried to introduce a foxhunt in Welford. Dennis Saville, his estate manager, had shot the vixen Michelle and Janie had been filming for another *Wildlife Ways* programme. Neither of the men were popular in the village. But as Mandy watched, she saw Mr Dickenson come out of the house and shake Sam Western's hand.

Mandy couldn't believe it. Suddenly, she felt a cold grip of fear in her stomach. 'Are you thinking what I'm thinking?' she said to James, fearfully.

'Uh-huh,' James nodded.

'Michelle?' Mandy asked.

'We'll have to wait and see, Mandy,' she replied, grim-faced. 'But it doesn't look good.'

Peter Dickenson, Sam Western and Dennis Saville began walking down through the paddocks towards them.

'Michelle, Janie, Mandy, James,' Mr Dickenson said, smiling half-heartedly, 'meet Mr Western, he's to be the new owner of Glisterdale Forest.'

Mandy and James were horrified. Their worst fears were realised. Sam Western completely ignored them and strode past, followed by Dennis Saville who was clutching a clipboard and a metal ruler.

'I'm sure he didn't mean to be rude,' Mr Dickenson said, watching Sam Western head off towards the forest. 'He seemed quite a charming man on the telephone. I'd better catch them up.'

'Wait!' Mandy called, catching Mr Dickenson's sleeve. 'Sam Western is a horrible man. He *hates* wildlife. He tried to start a foxhunt in Welford, and we saw him shoot a vixen bringing food to her cubs.' Mandy was almost in tears.

'He tried to poison our friend's goat,' James added, 'and he set traps to kill foxes which nearly caught Mrs Ponsonby's dogs.'

Mr Dickenson was visibly shocked. He looked to Michelle for confirmation and she nodded. He put his hand on his forehead. 'What have I done?' he muttered, shaking his head.

'You weren't to know what Sam Western was like,' Michelle said gently. 'And don't forget, you haven't much choice. But it could be very bad news for the wildlife.'

'What will happen to the deer now?' A tear slipped down Mandy's face as she spoke.

'Look, I *have* asked for a clause to be put in the contract that protects the wildlife.' Peter Dickenson reassured her. 'And as for the deer, because the whole of my estate is unenclosed they are free to go anywhere. Fortunately, they choose to stay. Deer are wild animals and as such have no owners. In open land like mine the deer are protected by wildlife acts.'

'But what if the land *is* enclosed?' Mandy worried, blowing her nose.

'If an estate is fenced they become the property of the landowner,' Mr Dickenson conceded. 'But don't worry, Mandy, I'll never enclose my land. As far as I'm concerned the deer can roam freely.' He managed a grin. 'I'm sure the deer will be fine. Look, Mr Western's coming back.'

'I think we'll have to tell him about the film we're making,' Michelle said, drumming her fingers on her binoculars.

Sam Western drew level with them on the way back to his Land-rover. 'Nice doing business with you,' he called to Mr Dickenson as he strode past. 'My lawyer will talk to yours.'

'Mr Western,' Michelle called, 'can I have a word please?'

Sam Western turned, looking annoyed.

'Hurry up, then, I'm a busy man.'

'It's just that I thought I should tell you we're making a film about the deer in Glisterdale Forest,' Michelle said. 'I wouldn't want you to think we were trespassing.' She laughed.

Sam Western stared at Michelle. 'That's out of the question,' he said curtly. 'My men will be down shortly to carry out a few jobs. You'll be in their way.'

Mandy looked at Peter Dickenson.

He was frowning now, and he stepped forward. 'Hold on just a moment, Mr Western,' he said crossly. 'It is still officially *my* land you know, and I gave these people permission to film the deer.'

Sam Western looked hard at Mr Dickenson. 'I don't want to jeopardise our arrangement,' he said cautiously, 'but I can't have people walking about willy-nilly. I've got plans for that forest.' He looked at Michelle. 'You can carry on until the work starts, young woman, and then I want you out!' He turned and strode off.

'Well!' Michelle exclaimed. 'He doesn't change.'

Mandy and James exchanged grim glances. 'What do you think his plans are?' Mandy asked Peter Dickenson.

'I don't know, Mandy, but we have to presume he'll want to make money out of it somehow,' Mr Dickenson answered. 'He hasn't told me his plans.'

'Then it's up to us to show everyone the importance of the forest in our film,' Michelle said firmly.

'And its value as a home to all the wildlife, especially the deer,' Mandy said.

'*Especially* the deer,' Peter Dickenson echoed softly, as he turned and walked back to the house.

Three

'Under the circumstances,' Michelle told them, 'I think we should do some more filming today. Let's get as much footage under our belts as we can before the workmen begin. Agreed?'

Mandy, James and Janie all nodded. 'OK. Let's go,' Michelle said, leading them back to the edge of the forest.

While Michelle and Janie discussed technical details, Mandy leaned against a huge oak tree and tried to calm down. She wished there was a way to persuade Sam Western to leave the deer alone.

'What do you think Sam Western's got in mind?' James asked.

Mandy shrugged. 'Who knows?' she replied. 'But knowing him, it won't be good. I just wish Mr Dickenson didn't have to sell the land at all.'

'Look, you two,' Janie said softly, interrupting their discussion. 'There are some does with fawns. See, just coming into the clearing.'

Mandy looked through her binoculars. 'There's Sprite!' she exclaimed under her breath. 'Look, James, the one at the front.'

'It looks like her,' James said, as he fiddled with the focus on his binoculars, 'but I'm sure that fawn has a tag. Look at her ear.'

'Oh yes,' Mandy said, her voice full of disappointment. With Sam Western threatening the deer's home, she was more anxious than ever to find the fawn and know that she was all right.

At about half-past six they packed up and made their way back to the house.

'We got some good shots,' Michelle said, making notes as she went along. 'You know, the change of ownership of the forest will give an extra twist to the programme.'

'It will be interesting to see exactly what "jobs" Mr Western's men are going to start on,' Janie said as they neared the house.

'Look,' said Mandy, pointing at the house. 'It's Mrs Dickenson.'

Mrs Dickenson was standing at the kitchen door, waving to them. 'Peter would like a word before you go, if you've time,' she said, holding the door for them. 'He's in the study.'

Mandy led the way along the oak-panelled hall to a large wooden door with a big brass handle that stood open.

Mr Dickenson was on the phone. He looked up and beckoned them to come in. 'Well, I'd like it on the record that I am extremely angry about it,' he was saying in a cold voice. 'In fact, I almost feel like suggesting you tear up that contract. Forget selling the land, I'll raise the money another way.'

Mandy swallowed hard and looked at Michelle, who was frowning.

'I am not being hasty,' Peter Dickenson went on. 'I want protection for the deer herd. In writing.' He listened for a few minutes then said calmly, 'Fine, that will be acceptable. Goodbye.' Putting the phone down he sat back with a sigh.

'Trouble with Sam Western?' Michelle asked.

'That was Western's solicitor,' Peter Dickenson told them. 'I wanted you to know that Western has demanded that they take out the contract clause protecting the deer and other wildlife.'

Mandy gasped. 'But you can't!' She looked from Mr Dickenson to Michelle. 'You know what will happen if the deer aren't protected. We can't trust Mr Western.'

'It's all right, Mandy,' Mr Dickenson said. 'I've insisted that he gives me written assurance that the deer can roam in the forest for as long as they want to; for ever, in fact.'

'That sounds reasonable,' Michelle said. 'I mean he can't change his mind, once he's promised.'

'Can't he?' James muttered to Mandy.

'He's a businessman, James. As long as I have his word, it will be all right,' Mr Dickenson said. 'I'm sure everything will be fine, now that we've sorted out the important issues.' He stood up and walked around the desk. 'There's a company coming tomorrow to give me a quotation for the work on the house. If we can agree on the price, they can start work this week. It will be a terrible upheaval, but the sooner the repairs are done, the better.'

'At least the house will be safe,' said Michelle. 'We'll carry on filming tomorrow, then, if that's convenient?'

'Be my guest,' Peter Dickenson told her, as he walked them to the front door.

They piled into the Jeep and Michelle set off. At the gates she stopped and looked both ways. A huge, dirty truck was approaching. The driver flashed his lights to let Michelle pull out. But as they turned out of the drive, Mandy saw the driver of the truck clearly.

'It's Dennis Saville!' she gasped in alarm.

'And his workmen,' James added, looking back.

Mandy turned to watch and her heart

thudded as she saw them turn into Glisterdale Grange. James shook his head.

'I hope they're not planning to start work already,' Michelle said, concern in her voice. 'The contracts haven't been exchanged yet.'

Mandy frowned. The deer were at Sam Western's mercy and now it seemed that the *Wildlife Ways* programme was too.

'See you tomorrow, Mandy,' Michelle called, as Mandy jumped out of the Jeep at Animal Ark. 'And try not to worry too much about the deer. Sam Western's giving Mr Dickenson a written guarantee, don't forget.'

Mandy nodded and gave a weak grin. But as she entered the cottage she couldn't shake off a feeling of impending doom.

Adam Hope was sitting in the armchair in the kitchen reading some veterinary papers. 'What's up love?' he said, putting down the papers. 'I can tell you're worried. Has something happened at the Grange?' He patted the arm of the chair. 'Come on, come and tell your old dad all about it.' He gave her one of his lopsided grins.

'Dad, it's awful!' Mandy said, going over to perch on the edge of the armchair. 'Mr

Dickenson *has* sold the forest, and guess who's bought it?'

Adam Hope looked shocked. 'I really didn't think he would sell,' he said. 'Things must be pretty bad for him. So who *is* the new owner?'

'Sam Western,' Mandy said in a miserable voice.

'Oh, I see.' Her dad frowned. 'Not the sort of person I would imagine wanting a deer forest.'

'That's what I'm worried about, Dad,' Mandy said urgently. 'He's sent some workmen up there already. What do you think he's up to?'

'I don't know. What does Peter say about it all?' he asked. 'I'm sure he wouldn't do anything to endanger the deer.'

'Mr Dickenson's made him put it in writing that the deer can stay in the wood,' Mandy said doubtfully.

'There you are then, love,' Adam Hope smiled. 'That sounds fine. Like I said, Peter will look after the deer. He enjoys having them there so much that he doesn't even like it when they have to cull them.'

'Cull them?' Mandy asked warily. 'What do you mean?'

Her father sighed. 'Well, to start with, did you know that deer have no natural predators in

Britain, now that wolves have been wiped out?' he began. 'Apart from dogs and the occasional road casualty, there's nothing to keep down the deer numbers,' he continued.

'But why *should* their numbers be kept down?' Mandy asked, shocked. 'They're beautiful animals, why can't they grow old and die naturally?'

'Even a forest as big as Glisterdale can only support so many deer,' her dad explained. 'If the deer population grows too big, then you get too many animals competing for too little food. That's not good for the deer or the land.' Mr Hope looked up into Mandy's face. 'Think about it, love. the deer at Glisterdale are very successful. But you have to remember all the other wildlife in the forest. The deer can't keep breeding out of control, can they?'

Mandy knew her dad was right, but that didn't mean she had to *like* it. 'So how do they cull them?' she asked.

'They shoot any obviously old or sick animals, although it's quite hard to pick them out,' Adam Hope explained gently. 'And they usually shoot some of the does.' He put his hand up to stop her interrupting. 'It has to be done, Mandy, even if we don't like it.'

'Does Mr Dickenson do the culling at Glisterdale Grange?' Mandy asked.

'No,' Mr Hope said. 'It has to be done in season and by a professional using a rifle. As Glisterdale Grange isn't large enough to have a deer-keeper, Tony Morris does it.'

Mandy didn't like the thought of it one bit, but she knew her dad was right. You couldn't let the herd get too big. She was glad that Mr Dickenson didn't have to shoot them himself, though.

'What happens to the dead ones, Dad?' Mandy asked quietly.

'I thought you might ask that,' Adam Hope said, looking at her seriously. 'In an ideal world, Mandy, deer would be able to run free. But you have to think of it as harvesting a food source, like any other. Just like Mr Masters has chickens, Glisterdale Grange has deer.' He looked at Mandy to make sure she understood. When Mandy nodded, Adam Hope continued. 'A game dealer will buy the deer from Peter. It's my bet that any money he gets, Peter Dickenson ploughs back into the herd.'

'What do you mean?' Mandy asked, puzzled.

'Well, deer can be expensive to keep. They may be wild animals but they still need extra feed in the winter, to keep up their strength through the cold months.'

'So Mr Dickenson might use the money to buy hay or something?' Mandy asked, feeling sure that Mr Dickenson was doing something to help the deer.

'Well, I imagine he probably buys in some concentrates, food pellets and carrots, things like that,' Mr Hope told her.

'Dad!' Mandy said as the thought struck her. 'What do you think Sam Western will do about culling the deer?'

'If he's said the deer can stay, I would imagine things will continue much as they are.' Mr Hope stood up and ruffled Mandy's hair. 'There may be no reason at all for you to worry,' he told her. 'Sam Western's a greedy businessman, he probably just can't resist buying up any land that's going. He might not even have any solid plans for it yet.'

There was a crunch of gravel as the Animal Ark Land-rover pulled up outside. Mandy and her dad heard the car door slam and Mrs Hope's key in the lock. 'Hi,' she called. 'I'm just popping into the surgery, I'll be back in a minute.'

'Whoops!' Adam Hope said, striding over to

the fridge. 'I promised to make a start on dinner.'

'I'll lay the table,' Mandy offered, jumping up. 'Shall we eat indoors or in the garden?'

'Inside, Mandy, I still haven't mended that table-leg and I promised Mum I'd do it today!' Adam Hope said guiltily, giving her conspiratorial look.

By the time Emily Hope had come back from unpacking her vet's bag in the surgery, the kitchen was a hive of activity. Adam Hope was mixing oil and vinegar to make a salad dressing and Mandy was slicing tomatoes. The smell of warm bread filled the air.

'Hi, you two,' Emily Hope said, dropping a kiss on Mandy's cheek. 'How did the filming go?'

Mandy told her mum all about Sam Western buying Glisterdale Forest.

'I expect,' her mother said, taking a quiche from the fridge and removing the foil, 'he probably sees it as an investment to sell on later.'

'That's just what Dad said,' Mandy said, surprised.

'There you are,' Adam Hope told her with a grin. 'Great minds think alike!'

'So don't worry too much about the deer, Mandy,' her mum said. 'I know you where animals are concerned.' She sat down at the table. 'It's a beautiful evening, why aren't we eating outside?' she asked, glancing sideways at Mr Hope. 'Adam?'

'We decided it was too cold, actually,' Mr Hope said innocently. 'Didn't we, Mandy?'

Mandy nodded, trying to suppress a grin. The warm evening sunlight was streaming through the kitchen windows.

Mandy loved evenings like this when they were all together, and nobody was out on a call. Maybe Mum and Dad were right and everything at Glisterdale Grange was going to be fine. Maybe Sam Western *had* had a change of heart when he agreed to protect the deer. She couldn't wait for the next day to carry on with the filming.

Mandy and her dad offered to clear away after supper, so Emily Hope could go and relax with the paper. They washed up in silence, both deep in thought. Mandy's mind wandered to Glisterdale Grange and the beautiful deer they had been watching that day. But then an awful thought struck her. Her dad had said 'usually they shoot some of the does'. Sprite was a doe!

Mr Dickenson would recognise Sprite but Sam Western's men might shoot her!

'Dad!' she exclaimed, dropping the tea towel she was holding. 'What about Sprite? If there's a cull, I mean?'

'They usually cull in November, Mandy. Sprite's much too small, so don't worry,' Mr Hope told her.

'But what about next year?' Mandy asked, anxiously. 'She'll be much bigger then.'

Adam Hope looked at his daughter's pale, worried face. 'Even next year, Mandy, they'll still be able to tell last year's fawns. Why don't you ask Peter Dickenson first thing in the morning?' he suggested.

'OK,' Mandy agreed, hoping her dad was right. She picked up the tea towel and carried on drying the plates. Her dad had made her feel a bit better but she still couldn't help worrying. If only Peter Dickenson had been able to keep Glisterdale Forest. She was sure Sprite would have been safe with him.

Four

'*All things bright and beautiful, all creatures great and small . . .*'

The words boomed through the air. Mandy turned over in bed and smiled to herself. It was her dad's favourite hymn from the church choir and he loved singing it. But he could only remember the first verse, and after that he always got in a muddle. She listened as he continued singing.

'*The purple-headed mountain, the river running by . . .*'

Mandy giggled softly. This was the bit he always got wrong.

'*The sunrise and the morning that lightens up*

the sky.'

Mandy jumped out of bed, ran across the landing and banged on the bathroom door.

Adam Hope opened the door wearing his dressing-gown, toothbrush in hand.

'I know, I got it wrong!' he said grinning. 'One day maybe I'll get it right.' Mandy's dad sighed with a staged grimace.

'It's *sunset*, not sunrise,' Mandy told him, as he turned back to the basin. 'Dad, do you mind if I give Mr Dickenson a call?' she asked. 'I can't wait until we get over there later.'

'All right, Mandy,' Adam Hope said, grabbing a towel. 'I don't suppose we'll get any peace until you do.'

'Thanks, Dad,' Mandy called, as she ran down the stairs two at a time. Her dad knew her too well.

'Good morning, Glisterdale Grange,' Peter Dickenson said, answering the phone.

'Mr Dickenson, it's Mandy Hope here.' Mandy took a deep breath. 'Bert told us that Sprite would be running with the herd now and Dad's told me all about deer culling, and I wondered how . . .' she didn't have to finish her sentence.

'How we can recognise Sprite, do you mean?'

Peter Dickenson cut in. 'I'm really sorry, Mandy, didn't I tell you? In all the confusion yesterday, I completely forgot.'

'Tell me what?' Mandy pleaded.

'Well, some time ago when the herd came near the house, Tony and I caught Sprite and I tagged her,' he explained. 'Sprite has a neat little blue ear tag in her right ear to identify her. There's no other way you'd know her once she's running free.'

Mandy felt relief flood through her. She was now certain that the fawn they'd seen with an ear tag *was* Sprite.

'Oh, I'm so pleased, Mr Dickenson,' Mandy said. 'I thought I spotted her yesterday but I didn't know she was tagged.'

'I'm sure it was her, you'd probably still recognise her,' Mr Dickenson replied. 'Aren't you coming over today?'

'Oh yes,' Mandy said. 'I just couldn't wait any longer to find out.'

'That's OK, Mandy,' Mr Dickenson told her. 'See you later on then. Goodbye.'

'Bye,' Mandy said, putting the phone back.

'Well?' said Adam Hope coming down the stairs. 'You look happier now. I gather Sprite is tagged.'

Mandy nodded as they walked together into the kitchen. Emily Hope was just rinsing her cereal bowl in the kitchen sink.

'I heard the good news, too. Mandy. That's great.' Mrs Hope put her bowl on the draining-board, then picked up her keys and went to the back door. 'I promised to pop up to the animal sanctuary. The cat that had the breech birth last week isn't doing too well. When are you off to meet Michelle?'

'In about twenty minutes,' Mandy said, pouring her dad some orange juice. 'I said I'd walk down and meet the others in the village.'

'I'll see you tonight then.' Emily Hope blew them both a kiss and went out.

After breakfast, Mandy cleared the table and washed up. She stacked the dishes in the cupboard and popped into the surgery to say goodbye to her dad.

Simon had just arrived and in reception Jean was busy answering the phone. Just for a moment, Mandy regretted not being able to stay. While she loved helping out on *Wildlife Ways*, she *did* miss the patients at Animal Ark.

'We'll still be here next week when the

filming's finished,' her dad said, noticing the wistful look on her face.

'And so will all your jobs, Mandy,' Simon said, '*and* all the extra jobs you've promised to do for me!'

'I'm gone!' Mandy laughed, racing out of the door and sprinting up the lane.

In the Jeep she told the others about Sprite.

'Phew, that's a relief,' James said. 'So that fawn we saw *was* Sprite.'

'With luck you might see her again today,' Michelle said. 'I'm hoping to get some footage in the open today.'

'Could you bring that tripod for me, please, James?' Janie asked, as they unloaded the equipment.

They set up the camera between the paddocks and the forest, weighting down the feet of the tripod with three large stones to hold it steady. Janie pointed the camera towards the path that led into the forest and they settled down to wait.

Mandy was the first to spot the herd of deer emerging from the forest, browsing on oak leaves as they passed. She and James counted them.

'Fourteen!' Mandy said, softly. 'One male with enormous antlers—'

'And two with little dumpy stubs,' James noted.

'The male with the large antlers will be quite old,' Michelle explained. 'You see the broad, flat parts on the end of its antlers? They're called the "palms", and only moose and fallow deer have them. Each year the bucks grow bigger antlers.' She looked through her binoculars. 'He's still got some velvet hanging on the right antler, can you see it?'

'Yep, I can see it,' James said, studying the buck. 'Why *do* deer shed their antlers, Michelle?' he asked. 'Why don't they just grow bigger and bigger?'

'Once an antler is fully-grown and has shed its velvet, what's left is actually dead bone,' she replied. 'Every year, around May and June, the bucks start to shed their antlers. Each year they grow a bigger set, sort of in line with how old they are growing.'

'And do they start growing another set immediately?' Mandy asked.

'Yes, and they grow covered with the velvet,' Michelle told them.

'What's the velvet for?' quizzed James.

'The antlers need air and food to grow,' Michelle said. 'The velvet is a special sort of skin that helps to supply everything the bone needs.'

'And you said once the antlers are fully grown the velvet comes off?' James asked.

'That's right, James, and then the blood supply is cut off. The antler can't grow any bigger and it dies,' Michelle said, laughing at his expression.

'It seems a complicated way of growing antlers.' James grinned.

'How absolutely fascinating!' exclaimed a voice behind them.

They spun around to find Mrs Ponsonby standing there, Pandora, her Pekinese in her arms, and Toby, the little mongrel, dancing at her feet. 'You must be Michelle Holmes, from *Wildlife Ways*. My dear, *such* knowledge. I am delighted, no, *honoured* to meet you,' she announced, holding out a gloved hand.

Michelle looked rather shocked. They had all been so absorbed in watching the deer that none of them had heard Mrs Ponsonby coming. Michelle took her hand and shook it. 'And you are . . . ?' she asked.

'Amelia Ponsonby, dear, and this is Pandora

and that is Toby,' Mrs Ponsonby told her, putting the Pekinese on the ground. Mandy noticed that both dogs had bright new collars. Toby's was red and yellow tartan and Pandora's was pink and studded with tiny sparkling stones.

'Hello, Mrs Ponsonby,' Mandy said, bending down to stroke Pandora.

'Good morning, Mandy and James,' Mrs Ponsonby replied. 'I'm pleased to see you are hard at work making your film.'

Mrs Ponsonby was rather over-dressed for the woodland setting. She wore a flowered dress with a little matching jacket and the brim of her straw hat was pinned up at the front with a bunch of deep red plastic cherries. 'Now, dear, you just carry on as before and we will watch quietly,' she told Michelle. 'We'll be as quiet as mice, won't we, precious?' she cooed, gathering up Pandora and shuffling over towards Janie.

'What is happening here?' Michelle asked Mandy in a low voice. 'What does she think she's doing?'

'She probably wants to be in the film,' Mandy guessed.

'Huh!' Michelle exclaimed. 'We'll see about that.' She turned towards Janie who was standing with a bemused look on her face while

Mrs Ponsonby peered through her camera.

'Utterly fascinating,' Mrs Ponsonby was saying. 'How very exciting it all is,' she said. 'Now don't let me get in your way,' she added, standing back.

For several moments she stood quietly behind them, while they watched a young doe approaching. Then, as the deer drew very near to them and Janie began to film, Mrs Ponsonby announced, 'I loved your programme last week, dear,' in a loud voice. 'And we always listen to your radio slot too, don't we, precious?' she said to Pandora. The doe fled in panic.

Michelle turned to Mrs Ponsonby, frowning,

and put her finger to her lips.

'Oops, sorry,' Mrs Ponsonby whispered, shaking her head so that the cherries on her hat wobbled precariously.

Mandy and James exchanged glances as Janie began filming again.

In the forest a deer barked and another answered. The buck with the big antlers and his group were just coming into view again when, suddenly, Janie switched off the camera and turned to Michelle. 'It's no good, I'm picking up a strange noise on the sound recording,' she said in a worried voice. 'It sounds like someone breathing heavily. I think we'd better move position.'

Together Janie and Michelle carried the camera and tripod nearer the forest and resumed filming.

But after just a few seconds Janie stopped again. 'It's no good, I'm still getting that noise.'

'Right,' Michelle decided, 'we have to find out what it is. Everybody keep absolutely still.'

Mandy and James, Michelle and Janie and even Mrs Ponsonby froze like statues. They all heard the panting noise.

'Herh, herh, herh.' Eyes wide, Pandora puffed

away, getting faster now that everyone was looking at her.

'Pandora, darling, do be quiet,' Mrs Ponsonby hissed under her breath.

'Oh, poor Pandora, she can't help it,' Mandy exclaimed, stroking the little dog's head.

'Don't worry, I'll make sure she stops,' Mrs Ponsonby promised confidently.

'I'd appreciate that. Otherwise, I'm afraid I shall have to ask you to take her away,' Michelle replied apologetically.

But Mrs Ponsonby's attempts to silence Pandora by rocking her gently in her arms didn't work. In fact, it made Pandora's noisy breathing worse. Just at a crucial moment came a loud 'hic' followed shortly by another one. As well as panting, Pandora now had hiccups.

Michelle turned and looked at Mrs Ponsonby.

'I'll take her for a little walk, shall I, dear?' she asked Michelle.

'What a good idea!' Michelle said with a firm nod. 'Keep the dogs on leads though, we don't want them chasing the deer,' she called after Mrs Ponsonby.

Mrs Ponsonby looked as if she had been struck in the face. 'My dogs would not *dream* of chasing deer. They are far too well brought up,' she said with a haughty expression.

Mandy and James turned away to stifle their laughter as Mrs Ponsonby flounced off. But she hadn't given up yet. When she reached the forest, she walked the dogs up and down, up and down, peering every so often in the direction of the camera.

'Oh no, what's she playing at?' Janie complained.

'She's trying to get in the film,' Mandy told her with a grin. 'She's very determined.'

'Not as determined as me!' Michelle exclaimed. 'Stop filming and swing the camera round, Janie,' she ordered. 'OK, everyone, let's turn around and pretend to film in another direction.'

Mandy peeked over her shoulder. After a few minutes, Mrs Ponsonby gave up and disappeared into the forest.

'She's gone,' Mandy told them, stretching her arms above her head.

'I think we'll take a break now anyway,' Michelle said. 'We need a volunteer to go back to the Jeep for the picnic.'

'I'll go,' James offered, taking the keys Michelle held out to him.

'I'll come with you.' Mandy was eager to

stretch her legs a bit. 'Trust Mrs Ponsonby to turn up like that!' she said, as they walked up the path toward the paddocks. 'Hey, look, James, what's that?'

Stacked in piles beside the gate to the paddocks were huge rolls of chain-link fencing, wrapped in thick polythene.

'Mr Dickenson must be planning some work,' James said, as they climbed over the gate. 'Race you to the car park!'

They were neck and neck as they neared the car park but James surged ahead and touched down just before Mandy. 'That's the second time I've beaten you,' he told her. 'I must be getting faster.'

James unlocked the Jeep and between them they carried the refreshments back to the others.

Michelle poured coffee for herself and Janie, and handed Mandy and James cans of soft drinks. Janie opened a packet of chocolate digestive biscuits that were beginning to melt and stick together. They were all munching the biscuits when James spotted Mrs Ponsonby heading back towards them with the dogs.

'I won't disturb you,' she said. 'I'll be taking my two darlings home soon, they're getting rather hot.' She was red-faced and puffing from the effort of her walk. 'I just wanted to show you what we found in the forest. Look, a bird has picked it clean. I thought you might want to take a picture of it for your programme.'

'May I see?' Michelle asked. Mrs Ponsonby handed her the remains of a pine cone. 'That's a squirrel's work,' Michelle told them. 'Squirrels eat pine cones rather like we eat corn on the cob. They strip it bare.' She held up the cone to show them all. 'A bird would have just pecked out the seeds and left it looking rather ragged.'

Mrs Ponsonby looked very impressed. 'Such knowledge, dear,' she said approvingly.

At that moment Peter Dickenson came striding down the path. 'How are you getting on here?' he asked. 'Seen lots of deer?'

'Loads,' Mandy told him, 'and Mrs Ponsonby found a pine cone that the squirrels have eaten.'

Mr Dickenson's eyes lit up. 'Ah yes,' he said, 'I meant to tell you about that. Did you know we have one of the few surviving pockets of red squirrels here?'

'Really?' Michelle exclaimed. 'When did you last see them?'

'Let me think. I haven't actually seen them for a few months,' Mr Dickenson said, scratching his head. 'But I saw them back in the spring.'

'They're really rare, aren't they?' Mandy asked, her voice full of excitement at the thought that they might spot a red squirrel.

James nodded. '*Really* rare!' he agreed, 'I'd love to see one.'

'Well, the pine cone proves they are still here, surely?' Mrs Ponsonby said.

'Sadly it doesn't,' Michelle said, shaking her head. 'It could mean that grey squirrels have moved in. We don't know why exactly, but the reds always move out when the greys move in.'

'There are definitely grey squirrels in Welford,' James told her.

'Ernie Bell's squirrel, Sammy, is a grey,' Mandy said. 'And we get lots in the garden.'

'Well, I suggest we all keep our eyes peeled to see if the red squirrels are still at Glisterdale,' Michelle decided. 'I'd love to get some shots of them for the programme and it might help us to protect the forest.'

'In that case, I shall come back tomorrow, dear,' Mrs Ponsonby told Michelle. 'To help you look. Bye-bye for now.'

As Mrs Ponsonby headed back towards the house, a group of workmen in overalls and hard hats were coming down the track carrying the rolls of chain-link fencing between them. Two men pushed wheelbarrows loaded with tools and bags of sand and cement, and another carried long, sharply pointed metal poles. 'Mind your backs, ladies and gentlemen,' a voice called out.

'Would you mind telling me where you are going with all that fencing?' Mr Dickenson asked, sounding puzzled.

Mandy frowned. If the men weren't working for Mr Dickenson they must be working for Sam Western – and that might mean the end of the filming . . .

Five

'Sorry if we disturbed you,' one of the workmen said, putting down his load. 'We're starting work fencing off the forest.' He gestured to Glisterdale Forest with his arm.

Peter Dickenson's face went white. 'On whose instructions, might I ask?' he said angrily.

'Instructions from the foreman,' the younger man replied, shrugging his shoulders. 'The foreman wants a fence, we make him a fence.'

'But this is *my* land,' Mr Dickenson said, 'and I don't know anything about this. I insist that you wait until I've found out what's going on. I am sure there's been a mistake.'

The workman looked doubtful. He glanced

back the way he'd come. 'Here comes Harry now, sir, he's the foreman. You'd best speak to him.'

'Good afternoon,' Peter Dickenson said, stepping out to greet the foreman.

'Afternoon, sir.' Harry was a big man with a dark suntan and his bald head was shiny and as brown as a conker. He stopped and shook Mr Dickenson's hand. 'What can I do for you?' he asked courteously.

'Perhaps you can tell me what's going on,' Peter Dickenson said, with a smile. 'I own Glisterdale Grange.'

'Ah!' Harry said. 'Then you'd be,' he looked at the worksheet pinned to his clipboard, 'Mr Western.'

'No, I'm Peter Dickenson,' he exclaimed. 'The owner of Glisterdale Grange.'

'Just a moment, sir,' Harry said, determinedly. 'I have been hired by a Mr Western to supervise the fencing of this forest. Are you telling me it doesn't belong to him? I wouldn't want to get involved in anything dodgy.'

'Well yes, Sam Western is buying the forest,' Peter Dickenson grudgingly had to admit. 'But I didn't know he intended to fence it off.'

'With all due respect, sir,' Harry said politely. 'If it's his forest, he can do what he likes with it.' He nodded to the startled group and started walking off towards the younger workman. 'Come on, Steve, let's get to work.'

Mandy couldn't bear it any longer. She was determined to find out what was going on. 'Excuse me,' she said, stepping forward. 'But *why* is he fencing it?'

'To keep people out, I expect. That's the usual reason,' Harry answered, turning back.

'Good Lord, the man doesn't waste any time,' Peter Dickenson said in a cold voice.

'I'm to fence all the areas where the public can get into the forest,' Harry told them. 'According to Mr Saville, he wants to keep out all the busybodies, all the "Nosey Parkers" who might start complaining when the work begins.'

'What work?' Mandy asked in a tense voice. At least Harry seemed happy to tell them anything, even if Sam Western wasn't.

'The tree felling. From what I've heard, he's going to start taking out the prime timber first,' Harry began.

'What's prime timber?' James asked, puzzled.

'Prime timber is the big old oaks and the fine beech trees,' Peter Dickenson told them quietly.

'The big trees that make up most of the forest.'

Mandy was shocked. She looked at James. Like her, he seemed to be having trouble taking it in.

'That's right,' Harry continued. 'He's got a mate who owns timber yards, apparently. Shame really.' He looked around. 'It looks like a nice forest for bird-watching. I'm partial to a bit of that.' He shrugged and said, 'Still, once the work starts with chainsaws, and the trucks and heavy machinery come in, you can't have people walking about. It's too dangerous. See you later!' And with a cheery wave he strode down the track.

'Sam Western has *got* to be stopped,' Mandy declared, horrified at the idea of the forest being felled. 'But how?'

'We'll have to find a way to change his mind, Mandy,' Peter Dickenson said. 'But first, I have to check on that fencing.' He strode off after Harry and Steve.

'You two go with him,' Michelle told Mandy and James. 'See what happens. Did you get all that, Janie?' she asked, turning to face her.

Janie nodded. Mandy turned to look at Janie and realised that, without any of them noticing, she had filmed the whole episode.

'Come on, James,' Mandy said, dashing after Mr Dickenson with James hot on her heels. When they caught up with him, he was inspecting the fencing. The workmen, with their hands on their hips, stood in a line behind it.

'Look, I know you are working for Sam Western,' Mr Dickenson was saying, 'but believe me, this fencing is nowhere near high enough.'

'It's nearly two metres high,' Harry said in a reasonable voice. 'People won't get over that too easily.'

'I'm not worried about people,' Peter Dickenson explained. 'There's a large herd of deer in the forest and they'll try to jump that. If it's not high enough the danger is that they will get caught on it. The fence *must* be at least two metres, preferably two metres thirty,' he said. 'I'm afraid I have to insist on it.'

Harry the foreman looked as if he was going to argue, but then changed his mind. 'I see, sir,' he said with a sigh. 'It's going to raise the cost a lot. I don't think Mr Western will wear it.' He looked at Peter Dickenson, who showed no sign of giving in. 'All right, sir, leave it with me,' he said, taking out his mobile phone.

Mr Dickenson turned, and with Mandy and

James in tow, walked back up to where Michelle
and Janie were waiting.

'But if Sam Western fences the forest and the
deer are trapped inside,' James asked, 'won't
that mean they will belong to him?'

'Strictly speaking, yes,' Peter Dickenson said.
'But he's not allowed to trap them in on
purpose, and they may leave of their own
accord before the job is finished. They won't
like the noise and disruption of the fence being
built.'

'But what if they *don't* leave,' Mandy said,
worried. 'I mean, if he wants to cut the forest
down, what's he going to do with the deer?'

'Well, he could have them caught and sell
them off as live animals, or he could have
them all shot,' Mr Dickenson said bluntly.
'Unfortunately, if deer become enclosed,
you have to rely on the benevolence of the
owner.' He gave a bitter laugh. 'Sam Western,
benevolent! Somehow that seems unlikely.'

'But if the deer leave the forest, they'll be
safe from Sam Western, won't they?' Mandy
asked hopefully.

'The problem is, Mandy, where will they go?'
Mr Dickenson ran his hand through his hair.
'Glisterdale has been a deer park for over nine

hundred years. But once the noise starts they'll probably flee the forest.'

'Where do you think they will go?' Mandy asked with a catch in her voice.

'The most likely prospect is that many will run on to the roads and get injured or even killed by traffic,' Michelle said solemnly. 'Others will get on to the surrounding farmland and if they start eating the crops, that won't please too many farmers.'

'Any farmer has the right to shoot deer on his own land if they cause problems.' Peter Dickenson sighed.

'So the only answer is to stop Sam Western from fencing the forest,' Mandy said fiercely. 'We *have* to find a way of saving the deer *and* the forest.'

'I have one idea, Peter,' Michelle said thoughtfully. 'If the forest is that old, then some of those oaks and beeches must be very old indeed.'

'I can look in the estate archives,' Peter Dickenson said. 'They would mention any preservation orders.'

'And we can ask around for more information about the forest,' Mandy offered. 'Lots of families have lived here for years and years. My grandad was born in Welford, he'll know something about the forest, I bet!' she said.

'We could look in the library at Walton as well,' James suggested. 'We *can* do it can't we? Find a way to save the deer I mean,' he said, turning to Michelle.

'We can certainly try,' Michelle agreed. 'And we can cover all this on *Wildlife Ways*. People will be very interested in the fate of the deer.'

'It would be awful if Sam Western got away with destroying the forest,' Mandy said. 'I bet that's why he's started work so quickly, before all the people he calls "Nosey Parkers" can stop him.'

'And by "Nosey Parkers" he means bird-watchers, ramblers, wildlifers and anyone else who enjoys the forest,' Michelle said angrily. 'Like us. The sort of people who would rightly complain.'

'There is another way I can stop him,' Peter Dickenson told them. 'At the moment, the only way he could bring heavy machinery in would be over my land.'

'And you could refuse him access!' Mandy was getting fired up now. 'But is there any other way he could get in?'

'There is a place where he could make a drive

from the main road,' Mr Dickenson said, 'but it would involve a lot of work and slow them down.'

'And he'd need to get planning permission, wouldn't he?' Janie added, dismantling the camera. 'That's not easy,' she pointed out.

'It is if you're Sam Western!' Mandy said darkly.

'He has *friends*,' James said. 'In high places.'

'We'll just have to block his every move,' Mr Dickenson said. 'I'm sure we'll find a way.'

They started back up the track towards the house. Michelle had decided that with the workmen making so much noise in the forest, there would be no more filming today. Mandy and James hung back. 'That horrible man wants to ruin everything!' Mandy said, her voice a mixture of anger and sadness.

'Just when we thought Sprite was safe,' James said. 'I can't even think about her running out on to the road.'

Mandy stopped abruptly. 'We can't let him do it, James,' she said firmly. 'We just can't!'

James nodded. 'Whatever it takes, we'll stop him,' he agreed.

They were quiet on the journey back to Welford,

each trying to think of ways to stop Sam Western from destroying the deer forest.

'I'd like to get to Glisterdale very early tomorrow,' Michelle said as she dropped them off. 'Before the workmen start. Say about seven?'

Mandy nodded. They might have a better chance of seeing Sprite early in the morning, she thought to herself.

'How about you, James?' Michelle asked. They all knew how he hated getting up in the mornings.

'Yep, fine,' James agreed immediately. Mandy smiled at her friend. She knew he would do anything to help the deer.

When Mandy got home, both her parents were out on call. She went and sat in the residential unit and picked up a Jack Russell puppy with an injured ear. He had a special collar round his neck to stop him scratching his wound. As she sat stroking the little dog, Mandy started telling him all about Sam Western and his terrible plans for the forest.

'And,' she said, putting the little dog back in his bed, 'James and I are going to stop him!' She bent over and settled the dog down.

'*Whoooo!*' Mandy looked up when she heard

the strange quivery noise. There was nobody about but it hadn't sounded like an owl. She leaned through the open door and went to investigate.

'*Whoooo!*' Mandy heard the noise again. 'Are *yooo* going to stop?'

Mandy folded her arms and grinned. 'Come out, Dad, I know it's you!' she called.

Adam Hope stepped out from behind the hedge. 'I thought it sounded very realistic,' he said, looking disappointed.

'It would have been the world's first talking owl, then!' Mandy exclaimed.

Adam Hope laughed, then frowned. 'Let me

guess,' he said. 'Might it be Sam Western who's upsetting you?'

'Dad, he's *awful*,' Mandy declared. 'He's fencing off the forest and cutting down all the trees. There won't be anywhere for the deer to go! But James and I have decided to stop him.'

'You know, Mandy, some people have no feeling at all for the countryside,' her father told her. 'Sam Western probably hasn't given the deer a thought. His main concern will be business. There's so much pressure to produce an income from the land.' Mr Hope shook his head. 'And there's a lot of money to be made. Sam Western won't care about where the deer go or what happens to them. I'm afraid it's down to people who care to worry about that.'

'People like us, you mean?' Mandy asked.

'That's right,' Mr Hope replied. 'People who are willing to stand up and fight for what they believe is right. To challenge what they think is wrong. Like you do, love.'

'Me?' Mandy said, eyes wide with surprise.

'Yes, you,' her dad said. 'Mum and I are very proud of the way you stand up for animals.'

Mandy linked her arm in her dad's as they walked down the garden. 'Mmm,' she wondered aloud. 'Who do you think I get that from? I can't think of anyone around here who might be passionate about taking care of animals.'

Mr Hope laughed. 'You're a chip off the old block all right, Mandy Hope,' he said.

The light went on in the kitchen and Emily Hope waved to them from the window.

'You'll find a way to beat Sam Western,' Mr Hope told Mandy, opening the kitchen door. 'The battle has only just begun!'

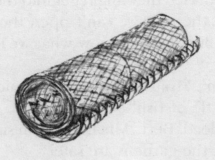

Six

Early next morning, as Michelle's Jeep pulled into Glisterdale Grange, Mandy could tell immediately that something was wrong. Estate workers were dashing about all over the place and there were deer wandering about in the car park.

Mrs Dickenson came running out to greet them. 'I'm glad you're here,' she told them. 'The deer have begun leaving the forest in quite large numbers. They don't like the disturbance. Most of them are in the paddocks but one or two came up on to the drive.' She looked over her shoulder at the sound of footsteps crunching on the gravel. 'Good, here comes Bert. I'm terribly worried they might get into the gardens and spoil them. If we can't open the grounds to the public, I don't know what we'll do,' she went on.

'Mornin', Mrs Dickenson,' Bert said. 'This is a nice kettle of fish!'

'It is indeed, Bert,' Mrs Dickenson sighed. 'Do you think the gardens are safe?'

'I reckon as I'd better walk around the ha-ha,' Bert said, 'just to be on the safe side.' He rubbed his back. 'Trouble is, me back's playin' up today. I might be a mite slow.'

'We could help,' Mandy offered quickly, looking across at Michelle. 'That's if you can spare us.'

'Of course, Mandy, that's fine,' Michelle said, glancing at Janie. 'We'll spend some time just filming the results of the night's events. Come down to the paddocks when you've finished.'

Mandy and James followed Bert to the gardens. A little way off they could see the paddocks. The lower one was dotted with deer mingling among the sheep. Mr Dickenson and Tony Morris were both standing by the fence watching. They waved to Mandy and James.

'Mr Dickenson's right worried,' Bert said, scratching his chin thoughtfully. 'And Mrs

Dickenson too. If them deer get into the gardens, we've had it. There'll be nowt for the visitors to see. Fact is, if they can't visit the house, nor walk in the woods, the garden's the only thing left.'

'When will the work start on the house?' James asked.

'Well, that's a bit of good news,' Bert said. 'Mrs Dickenson said they'll start spraying the east wing today, so the dry rot won't destroy the timbers. They can open that while the work's being done on the west wing.'

Bert stopped by a bridge that led over the ha-ha to the gardens. 'Right then, James,' he said. 'If you go inside the gardens and walk around checking the edge of the ha-ha, me and Mandy will check the inside wall.'

'What exactly am I looking for?' James asked.

'Look to see if the bank is crumbling anywhere,' Bert told him. 'Any place that a deer could use to get across.'

'What do *we* look for, Bert?' Mandy asked, looking at the steep inside wall of the ha-ha. It was built of bricks and looked solid and strong.

'We look to see if anything has fallen in,' Bert replied. 'You see up the back of the gardens, under those big trees?' He pointed at a stand of oak trees. 'A long time ago, some branches and leaves and debris fell down and almost filled the ha-ha to the top. I found a big old buck trying to climb across.'

Slowly they walked all around the gardens. Sure enough, at the far end, there was a pile of branches in the ha-ha and Mandy and James clambered down to clear it out.

'A deer might be tempted to try to cross on that,' Bert told them. 'Then it'd be in a pretty pickle.'

They continued around the garden and, when they reached the last bridge, they realised they had a serious problem.

'Look!' James cried. 'Someone's tried to break down the gate.'

'That's the deer that's done that,' Bert declared. 'They throw 'emselves at it, trying to break it down.' He tutted, shaking his head. 'They must have been in a panic to get away. It don't seem like they got in, though. It'll have to be fixed today.'

'What shall we do?' Mandy asked anxiously.

'We'd best get back and tell Tony Morris,' Bert replied, crossing the bridge into the gardens. 'He'll get someone up here to fix it. We'll go back through the gardens and check on my roses.'

They had just reached the pond when there was a loud screech. A peahen came hurtling down the path and stopped in front of James. She lay down at his feet and fixed him with one glinting eye.

'That's the same hen bird as before,' Bert said, grinning. 'She's after you, me lad.' The peahen wriggled and stared at James.

Bert was laughing fit to burst. 'Eh heh,' he gasped, wiping his eyes. 'You'll have to put a foot on her, lad, like the peacock 'ud do!' That sent him off into more fits of laughter.

Mandy couldn't help laughing too. James was blushing to the roots of his hair.

Suddenly there was a wail and a whoosh, and a big peacock ran up behind James and threw itself at his back.

Startled, James staggered forward, almost treading on the peahen at his feet.

'He's jealous!' Bert announced, grabbing James before he fell. 'What have you got that the hen likes so much?'

'Nothing!' James said, pushing his glasses back on and looking nervously around. 'I didn't do anything.'

They walked around the pond where the peafowl were drinking.

'Look out, lad!' Bert yelled as the big peacock fixed James with a menacing eye and started towards him again.

'Run, James!' Mandy cried.

James ran. The peacock followed him for a few paces. Then, as if it was content that James had been seen off, it strutted back to where Bert and Mandy stood. It stuck its brilliant blue chest out and lifted its tail-feathers, opening them out into a huge semicircular fan. The feathers were marked with eyespot patterns, and shimmered blue, gold and emerald green in the sunshine.

'Wow!' Mandy gasped in admiration at the sight. 'The patterns on his tail feathers are beautiful,' she said, awestruck.

'It's called his fan,' Bert told her. 'He's a beautiful bird all right.'

They walked over to where James waited at the bridge. It was still early and cool, but the sun was warm and he was taking off his jumper.

'For some reason that bird does *not* like me,' he said, falling into step as they walked back.

'But the hen bird does, young James.' Bert snorted and swallowed a laugh. 'Funniest thing

I've seen in a long time. She's taken a right shine to you!'

'James!' exclaimed Mandy. 'Your jumper. Look at the pattern on it.'

James held it out. 'Brown and blue circles,' he said wrinkling his nose. 'So what?'

'On a green background,' Mandy said with a grin. 'Look, Bert, it's just like the colours on the peacock's fan.'

'Aye, it is that,' Bert agreed. 'I reckon that peahen thinks you're a good-looking peacock,' he told James, spluttering with laughter again.

'Thanks a lot,' James said, grinning and blushing pink. 'That's just what I need!'

'There goes Mr Dickenson.' Bert noticed, pointing toward the house. 'Will you two do me a favour and tell him about the gate?' he asked. 'It'll save my poor old legs. I've plenty to do today as it is.'

'Of course we will,' Mandy said. 'Come on, James, we'll tell him about the gate and then we've got to meet Michelle.' They raced down to the house after Mr Dickenson and passed on the message.

By the time Mandy and James got to the upper paddock and met up with Michelle and Janie,

Sam Western's workmen had arrived.

'Morning,' Steve said, as he passed, pushing a wheelbarrow loaded with drums of water. 'We're cementing the posts in today.'

'Did you get the higher fencing like Mr Dickenson said?' Mandy asked.

Steve frowned and shook his head. 'Mr Western said his budget wouldn't run to it,' he told them, 'even though Harry explained it all to him. Mr Western doesn't care much for wildlife.'

'But isn't it dangerous for the deer?' asked James. 'They'll try to jump it and get hurt.'

Steve took off his hard hat and hung it on the barrow handle. 'I'll let you into a secret,' he said looking around. 'None of the lads are happy about the deer getting hurt by the fence. So, when we dig the channel that the chain link will sit in, we're going to make it a bit deeper than normal. That way we can keep the height down. I worked with deer once in Scotland,' he said. 'And they could *easily* clear a fence that was a metre and a half.'

'But the fawns won't be able to, will they,' Mandy sighed, thinking of Sprite.

'It's the best I can do,' Steve said. 'But don't forget, deer will only jump if they're under

pressure. Most of the time they'll follow the fence till they find a place to get out. In Scotland we once had a herd of deer that came across a fence too high to jump,' he said, grinning. 'A load of them charged at it over and over again until they just broke it down. I've never seen anything like it.'

'I've seen deer appear to test the height of a fence by standing up on their hind legs and touching the top with their chins.' Michelle told them.

'I've seen that too,' said Steve. 'If their chin touches the top, they'll jump it.'

'What did you actually do in Scotland?' Janie asked curiously.

'I was deer-keeper on an estate,' Steve said. 'Best job I've ever had.' He stared at the deer with a wistful look in his eyes. 'Ah well,' he said in a resigned voice, 'I'd best get back to work.' He headed off towards the forest.

'Oh no.' James glanced back towards the house. 'Look who's coming down the track.'

They all turned to look. Mrs Ponsonby was wearing a brown dress with big green swirly roses on it. On her head was a green straw hat with brown and beige silk acorns dotted around the brim. She didn't have her dogs with her and she looked very agitated.

'At least she's toned her colour scheme down,' Michelle observed dryly. 'That must be her idea of camouflage clothing!' Mandy tried not to look at James in case she started giggling.

'My dears, this is a dreadful state of affairs,' Mrs Ponsonby puffed as she hurried toward them. 'I've just heard from Mr Dickenson up at the house that Sam Western is fencing off the forest. It really is too, too dreadful.' She looked from Mandy to Michelle. 'Is there *no* curbing him?'

'We hope so, Mrs Ponsonby,' Michelle said calmly. 'We are going to do our very best.'

'Good,' Mrs Ponsonby said, nodding her head. '*I*, meanwhile, have a little idea of my own to follow up.' And she strode down the track towards the forest.

'What on earth is she up to?' Mandy asked, puzzled.

As they watched, Harry shouted something to Mrs Ponsonby and hurried over. He stood between her and the forest and held up his hands to halt her progress. But Harry was no match for Mrs Ponsonby on a mission. She marched past him, forcing him to jump out of her way. Before he had got over the shock of what had just happened she had disappeared among the trees.

'A formidable lady!' Janie exclaimed.

'Good job she's on our side, then, isn't it?' Michelle remarked. 'Oh look, there are more deer coming out of the forest. Can you film them, please, Janie?'

They stood watching in silence. First a buck with big antlers came out of the far end of the forest and looked cautiously around. Licking his nose to test the wind, he stamped first his right front foot and then the left.

'He's not too sure about being in the open,' Michelle said quietly. 'They're very unsettled by all the work going on.'

Suddenly the buck gave a series of barks. Five does, three fawns and another younger buck emerged from among the trees and joined him, jostling each other nervously. From behind them in the forest came a loud clang as one of the workmen up-ended a wheelbarrow, dumping a load of metal posts on the ground. In a flash, the deer were off. They ran straight up the paddock and then, to Mandy's amazement, one by one they began springing into the air, all four legs hanging straight down.

'That's called "pronking",' Michelle said.

'They do it when they're alarmed. For some reason, fallow deer do it more than any other type.'

'They're running at the paddock fence!' Mandy said, clutching her hand to her mouth. Effortlessly the group of deer leaped over the low wooden fence and slowed to a stop on the far side of the upper paddock. They put their heads down and began to graze.

'Cooee!' Mrs Ponsonby's voice broke the stillness. 'I've found the evidence.'

'What evidence?' Michelle said, turning around. Mrs Ponsonby was plodding up the track to where they stood.

'*This* evidence,' she said, holding a neatly chewed pine cone in one hand and a bag of acorns in the other. 'Red squirrels!' she declared. 'There are definitely red squirrels living in the forest.'

'I'm afraid the pine cone only tells us there are squirrels here,' Michelle said patiently. 'Not which species.'

'Ah, but there's more than that,' Mrs Ponsonby said confidently. 'I was reading about squirrels last night and red squirrels don't usually eat acorns, but grey squirrels do,' she explained. 'Here, I gathered a bag of young acorns. If grey squirrels were living in the forest, these would have been eaten.' She opened the bag and showed them all.

'Well, there wouldn't be very many acorns around,' Michelle agreed, 'but I don't really think this counts as proof. I'm afraid it's not substantial enough to prove that red squirrels are here.'

'What would you say if I told you I saw one?' Mrs Ponsonby challenged her triumphantly.

'Did you really?' Mandy asked, eyes wide with interest.

Mrs Ponsonby smiled smugly to herself.

'What did you see?' Michelle asked, doubtfully.

'Well, first I looked for coniferous trees for pine cones,' Mrs Ponsonby explained. 'And then I remembered that red squirrels like deciduous trees like oaks. So I found an old oak tree,' she continued, 'and, would you believe, as I stood there a red squirrel dropped a pine cone on my head. Well, of course, I looked up and there it was, as large as life and *so* pretty! It seems to have made its home in the fork of a branch.'

'It's called a drey,' James told her.

'That's the name for the nest squirrels make,'

Mandy explained. 'They make it out of twigs and leaves, and build a little roof over the top. Then they line it with thistledown and feathers.'

'Oh, how sweet,' Mrs Ponsonby said, smiling.

'And you're absolutely certain it was a red squirrel, not a grey?' Michelle asked carefully. 'They can look quite similar in summer,' she added tactfully.

'I can see you don't believe me, but I will very soon have some undeniable proof to show you,' Mrs Ponsonby announced, opening her handbag with a flourish and taking out a camera. 'You see, I took a photograph of it.'

'Oh, excellent, Mrs Ponsonby!' Michelle said, beaming at her. 'That will be *very* useful. If we can prove there's a pocket of red squirrels here, then they will be protected by law.'

Mandy glanced at James. He grinned back and she felt her spirits lift. Things were looking up.

'Good,' Mrs Ponsonby said. 'I shall go straight into town and get the film developed.' Dropping the camera back in her bag she marched off to her car.

'What a surprise! We're not out of the woods yet,' Michelle joked, 'but we're certainly on our way to building a case for saving the forest!'

'And the deer,' Mandy reminded her, in a firm voice.

Seven

'You're home early!' Emily Hope said, when Mandy and James arrived back at Animal Ark. 'I wasn't expecting you back till tonight.'

'Michelle and Janie wanted to do some editing,' Mandy told her. 'Michelle wants the deer film to be included in next week's programme.'

'So what are your plans for now, then?' her mum asked.

'We're going to work on saving the forest,' Mandy announced, 'if that's all right with you? We need to do some research. Mrs Ponsonby saw a red squirrel there this morning, and they're protected,' she told her mum.

'We thought we'd ask around,' James added, 'see if anyone knows anything about Glisterdale Forest that might help us to protect it.'

'I suppose we can spare you for a little bit longer,' Mrs Hope said, with a smile. 'Gran and Grandad arrived home from Scotland last night. Why don't you go and see them? They might have some ideas.'

'Good idea, Mum,' Mandy said, grinning at James. 'Gran might even have been baking today.' James went pink. Mandy was always teasing him about his liking for her gran's cakes.

'She probably has,' her mum said. 'It's her Women's Institute meeting tomorrow and they've got a produce sale on Thursday. Make sure you don't eat everything!'

Mandy and James headed up the lane to Lilac Cottage. A mouthwatering smell of baking drifted up the garden path. Mandy's grandad, Tom Hope, was in the greenhouse.

'Hi, Granded,' Mandy called, peeking inside. 'How was Scotland?'

'Hello, love!' he said. 'It was beautiful, apart from the midges!' he told her, holding out his arm to show the little red bite marks.

In front of him on the workbench inside the greenhouse were rows and rows of tiny flowerpots all with a single small plant in them. 'What are all those?' Mandy asked, puzzled.

'Don't they look smart? Like little rows of soldiers!' her grandad said, putting the last rooted cutting in the last pot and giving a big sigh of contentment. 'We've only been back a day and your gran's got me working. These are herbs to take to the WI sale. This is mint, those are rosemary . . .'

'And that's sage,' James said, pointing to a neat row of grey-green plants. 'We've got a huge bush in our garden.'

'That's right,' Grandad smiled. 'I'll just put them in trays and then we'll see if Gran can stop baking long enough to make us some tea.'

'Something smells wonderful,' Mandy said, handing James a polystyrene tray and holding up one herself.

'Gran was up at the crack of dawn making lemon curd and green tomato chutney,' her grandad told her, as he tidied up. James's eyes lit up and Mandy grinned. She knew James loved her gran's fresh lemon curd.

'That's us done,' Grandad announced, rubbing the potting compost off his hands. 'Put them over there in the shade, please, and let's go inside. Thirsty work, potting is.'

Inside Lilac Cottage the air smelled of coconut. Dorothy Hope was in the kitchen brushing little cakes with jam and rolling them in desiccated coconut. 'There, that's all the madeleines done,' she said out loud, putting the last cake on a tray. 'Hello, Mandy, James, I'm just about to make your grandad some tea.'

'You haven't put the cherries on top, Gran!' Mandy accused her. 'They don't look right.'

'Or the little leaves,' James added. 'Madeleines have to have leaves!'

'There now,' Gran said, smiling. 'I was saving those jobs for you, your mum said you might be down.' Handing them a tub of glacé cherries and a box full of little green angelica leaves, she added. 'You'll stop and have some tea, will you? I'll open a pot of your favourite lemon curd, James.'

'Wow, Gran!' Mandy exclaimed. 'You *have* been busy.'

On the dresser was a tray of jam tarts, a large chocolate cake, two carrot cakes and a big slab of her gran's special, rich, sticky parkin.

'That's not all, Mandy,' Dorothy Hope said, opening the oven and letting the delicious smell of baking bread waft through the kitchen. 'This is just about done, now it needs to cool awhile,' she said, taking the tin from the oven.

Mandy was busy dipping the cherries in jam and putting them on the top of the cakes while James added two leaves beside each cherry.

'Perfect!' Mandy announced, as they finished the last one. 'Grandad, can we ask you a question?' she said as he came back into the room. He had changed out of his gardening clothes and was wearing comfortable trousers and a clean blue shirt. He sat down at the table and turned his attention to Mandy and James.

'Fire away,' he said, taking a sip from his cup of tea. 'What can I do for you?'

'Well,' Mandy began, 'you know Glisterdale Forest, near where Mr Dickenson lives?' Mandy paused as her grandad nodded. 'Sam Western has bought it and he wants to cut all the trees down. We're looking for ways to stop him before all the deer leave.'

Gran was cutting great wedges of homemade bread and spreading them with butter and lemon curd. 'Your dad was telling us about that this morning,' she said sympathetically. 'It's terrible.'

'We thought you might know something about the forest that might help to stop him,' Mandy said.

'If I remember rightly, Mandy,' her grandad told her, 'Glisterdale Grange was taken over by the army during the war.'

'That won't help us,' Mandy said. 'It's nothing to do with the army now.'

'I remember that,' Gran commented, passing them plates and glasses of fresh orange juice. 'They used it for rifle training.'

'We used to cycle past there and hear the gunfire in the forest,' Mr Hope said. 'I tell you, we used to get a move on in case any of them were bad shots!'

'What were they shooting at?' James asked, a puzzled look on his face.

'They put targets on the trees,' Grandad said. 'The soldiers crawled through the long grass, where the paddocks are today, and fired at the targets.'

'But what's that got to do with saving the forest *now*, Grandad?' Mandy said with a frown. She couldn't see any connection, but there was a twinkle in her grandad's eye.

'Now there's a thought,' Gran murmured, taking a bite of bread. She chewed thoughtfully. 'If they used those trees as targets, won't they be full of bullets, Tom?'

'Your gran's right, Mandy.' Grandad nodded

agreement. 'Those trees wouldn't be any good for timber. They probably wouldn't even be any good for pulping.' He winked at Mandy. 'I bet Sam Western won't be too pleased to hear that!'

'That's great news, Grandad,' Mandy said, taking a piece of parkin from her gran. 'What about the big oak trees? Did they shoot at those?'

'No, not that I remember. Those big oaks are very old and Mr Dickenson's grandfather didn't want them damaged,' her grandad replied. 'They were only allowed to use the beech trees, mostly the ones nearest the house at that.'

'I bet the shooting frightened the deer,' James remarked.

'It certainly did, James,' Mandy's grandad said, 'but at that time some of the land next to Glisterdale Forest was woodland too and the deer moved right over the other side,' he told them. 'When I was a lad at school we were told that Queen Elizabeth I hunted deer in Glisterdale Forest,' he said, pausing to take a drink of his tea. 'In those days you needed the Queen's permission to cut off a single branch, never mind cut down a tree,' he said.

'So those oak trees could be over three hundred years old?' James asked thoughtfully.

'Surely that makes them pretty special!'

'I'll mention Sam Western's plans at the WI meeting tomorrow,' Gran said, gathering up the empty plates. 'Our members won't like it; they won't like it at all! There's too much chopping down of trees already, it's up to all of us to stop it.'

'The workmen have only just started fencing off the forest and the work is already frightening the deer,' Mandy sighed, picking up a cloth to help her gran with the washing up. 'They obviously don't feel safe and they've started coming out of the forest.'

'I hope Peter Dickenson's keeping an eye on those gardens. It would be sad if the deer got into them and destroyed them,' Grandad remarked, shaking his head at the thought.

'We're going to save the forest *and* the deer, Grandad,' Mandy told him. 'Come on, James,' she said. 'We'd better get on.'

Gran went to the larder and brought out a big plastic box. 'Here,' she said handing it to Mandy. 'I couldn't bake without saving something for your mum and dad.'

Mandy looked inside. 'Mmm, Dad's favourite carrot cake.' She kissed her grandparents. 'Thanks for the information,' she said.

'Yes, and thanks for the tea,' James added.

'Good luck with your campaign,' Grandad said, opening the front door for them. 'Gran's right you know, we're losing too many trees. We need the woodlands for the wildlife.'

'That would be a good slogan,' James suggested, as they started to walk back to Animal Ark. 'Woodlands for Wildlife!'

'Mmm,' Mandy agreed, but she was busy thinking about the great oaks. 'I'm going to phone Mr Dickenson and tell him what Grandad said as soon as we get in,' she declared. 'Then tomorrow we can visit Ernie Bell and Walter Pickard and ask them if they know anything about the red squirrels.' As head of Welford Wildlifers, Walter Pickard knew almost everything there was to know about the local countryside.

Adam Hope was putting some tablets in a bottle as they walked past the window of Animal Ark. Mandy lifted the lid and held up the box of cake so her dad could see. He gave her a thumbs up sign and licked his lips. In the kitchen James looked up the number of Glisterdale Grange while Mandy put the cake in the fridge.

'Here it is,' James called. He read the number out and Mandy dialled.

'Hello, Glisterdale Grange,' Peter Dickenson answered, after a few rings.

James stood close to Mandy, trying to hear.

'Mr Dickenson, it's Mandy Hope,' she said. 'I've got some news for you from my grandad.'

'And I've got some news for you, Mandy!' Peter Dickenson said. 'But let's hear yours first.'

Mandy told him about the beech trees being full of bullets. 'And Grandad thinks some of the oak trees are over three hundred years old.'

'He's right,' Peter Dickenson said. 'And what's

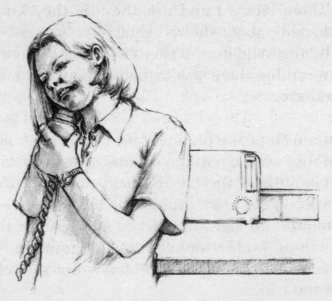

more, the County Council has confirmed that there are now preservation orders on all of them.'

'So Sam Western can't cut them down?' Mandy said, grinning at James, who punched the air with his first.

'No, Mandy,' Mr Dickenson confirmed. Mandy could hear the relief in his voice. 'He's not allowed to touch them.'

Mandy was still worried, though. 'Sam Western does exactly what he likes,' she said. 'What if he just cuts them down before anyone can stop him?'

'I don't think he will, Mandy, not this time,' Peter Dickenson told her. 'He'd be in big trouble if he went against the preservation order. The Council takes things like that very seriously. If he damages even one of those oaks, he could be liable for a massive fine. *That's* what will put Sam Western off now, the fear that it would cost him a lot of money. And if the beech trees prove to be useless to him, maybe he'll just decide to give up the idea of harvesting the timber.'

'I hope so,' Mandy said fervently. 'We've still got to make sure it's really safe for the deer, though.'

'And the squirrels,' James whispered to Mandy.

'And the red squirrels,' Mandy added.

'This is a step in the right direction,' Peter Dickenson assured her. 'Sam Western will have to change his plans.'

'But where are the deer now?' Mandy asked. 'Have they left the estate?'

'As soon as the workmen left, a lot of them made their way back into the forest,' replied Mr Dickenson. 'There's quite a large section that hasn't been fenced yet. And it's the actual work that frightens them, all that banging.'

'Then it's up to us to stop him before any *real* work starts,' Mandy said in a positive voice. 'The deer will *hate* it if Mr Western starts felling trees.' She swallowed hard.

There was a long silence on the other end of the phone. Then Peter Dickenson said in a sad voice. 'I know, Mandy. You can't imagine how many times I've been over and over the problem.' Sighing deeply he carried on. 'My only consolation is that I'm still here to care for them on the rest of the estate. Just suppose I'd had to sell the house as well, who knows what might have happened to the deer if we weren't around?'

Mandy shuddered at the thought of someone like Sam Western having the run of Glisterdale Grange. 'That's true,' she agreed.

'We'll all have to do the very best we can to keep them safe,' Peter Dickenson declared.

'Right!' Mandy agreed. 'Oh – and give Rosie a hug for me!'

'Yes, I will,' he answered, laughing. 'Bye for now.'

Mandy hung up the phone and looked out of the window at the sky. 'James, it won't be dark for ages yet,' she said. 'Why don't we go and see Ernie Bell and Walter Pickard now?'

'That's OK with me, it's on my way home anyway,' James replied. 'Mum's not expecting me back till later. I said I'd probably have tea here.' He grinned. 'I couldn't eat another thing after that tea over at your gran and grandad's.'

'I'd better just tell my mum first, then,' Mandy decided. With James following, she ran along the hall and pushed open the door to the Animal Ark reception. 'Is Mum busy, Jean?' she asked the receptionist.

Jean Knox pushed her glasses up on to her head and looked at Mandy. 'When *isn't* your mother busy, Mandy, tell me that?' she asked good-naturedly. 'She's in the examination room at the moment. One of the police dogs from Walton has got some glass in his paw.'

'Oh, poor thing!' said Mandy. 'Can we go in?' she asked, as the phone rang.

'I'm sure it will be all right,' Jean said, picking up the receiver. 'Good evening, Animal Ark. Yes, an appointment for when?' She fumbled with the appointment book. 'One moment please.' Putting her hand over the mouthpiece she scrabbled around under the desk.

'What have you lost, Jean?' Mandy said in a serious tone.

'My pen!' Jean hissed softly.

'Under that file,' Mandy whispered. How Jean ran the reception so efficiently with her poor memory, Mandy couldn't guess. She knocked on the door of the examination room.

'Come in,' Emily Hope called.

When Mandy opened the door she saw an enormous German shepherd dog sitting on the examination table. It watched Mandy and James enter with bright, intelligent eyes.

'All right, Gaffer, you'll be fine now,' Mrs Hope stroked his head.

The young policeman holding his lead grinned at Mandy. 'He thought he'd get time off work with a bad paw,' he joked. 'But Mrs

Hope's fixed him up perfectly.'

'A day's rest for that pad and he'll be fine. Won't you?' Mandy's mum said.

As Gaffer jumped down, Mandy stepped forward, looking at the policeman. 'Can I stroke him?'

'Sure,' he nodded vigorously. 'Gaffer's an old softie when he's off duty.'

Mandy and James made a fuss of the big dog while Mrs Hope gave his handler instructions on taking care of the injured paw.

'Pop back with him if there's any problem.' Emily Hope said, as the young policeman left. 'Now,' she turned expectantly to Mandy and James. 'What can I do for you two?'

'We're off to see Walter Pickard and Ernie Bell,' Mandy told her. 'To see if they know about the red squirrels at Glisterdale.'

'Fine, but make sure you're home before dark, please,' Emily Hope ordered, opening the door. 'And don't outstay your welcome if they're busy,' she added, with a smile.

'OK, we won't. Gran sent you a carrot cake,' Mandy called over to her. 'It's in the fridge.'

'Who shall we visit first, Ernie or Walter?' James said breathlessly, as they raced down the lane.

'Whoever we leave until last will be cross.' The two old men were always competing with each other, and each liked to think he knew more about the village.

'We'll decide that when we get there,' Mandy puffed, running across the green towards the pub and the row of cottages behind, where Ernie Bell and Walter Pickard lived. But as they reached the Fox and Goose, Mandy grabbed James's sleeve and stopped.

'Looks like our problem's solved,' she smiled. 'Look!'

Eight

Sitting at a wooden table outside the pub were Ernie Bell and Walter Pickard, both in shirt-sleeves with flat caps on their heads. 'Come on, let's go and see them.' Mandy said.

'Good evening, Walter, Ernie,' James said politely, hovering beside the table.

'Hello, young James, young Mandy,' Walter said in his gruff voice. 'And how's life treating you?'

'We've got a campaign on at the moment,' Mandy announced, pulling a couple of chairs over. 'That's why we wanted to see you both.'

'Oh aye,' Walter said, raising his eyebrows quizzically and pushing back his cap. 'Happen you've struck lucky then. Two for the price of one.'

'How's Sammy?' Mandy asked Ernie Bell.

'He's on a diet!' Ernie pronounced darkly. 'Some folks,' he said, looking pointedly at Walter, 'have been giving him too many treats.'

'One cream cracker won't hurt him,' Walter spluttered. 'It's all them nuts!'

'Have you ever seen red squirrels around here?' Mandy said, tactfully changing the subject.

'Not nowadays, lass.' Walter shook his head slowly from side to side. 'Happen there's still some left, but not in Welford, not where you find the grey. Never find the two together.'

'Why the interest in red squirrels?' Ernie asked bluntly. 'What's wrong with grey?'

'Oh no, nothing,' Mandy said hurriedly. 'It's just that we're trying to save the forest at Glisterdale. We think there might be red squirrels there, and if there are it might help protect the forest because they're so rare.'

'I heard Sam Western had bought the forest,' said Walter. 'He's causing trouble again, is he?'

'He wants to cut down the forest,' Mandy told them, and began to explain about the danger to the deer. 'We need to find a way to stop him destroying their home.'

'Protected by law, red squirrels are,' Walter Pickard said, nodding.

'Mrs Ponsonby is sure she saw one at Glisterdale,' James said.

'Pah!' Ernie Bell retorted. 'It was probably just a grey in the sunlight.'

'I'd agree with Ernie here,' Walter said. 'They can look alike in summer. Even country folk can have a job telling 'em apart.'

'That's what Michelle said,' Mandy told them, disappointed. 'But we're really hoping Mrs Ponsonby is right.' Mandy was determined to keep positive.

'You might be in luck, now I think about it.' Walter rubbed his chin. 'Glisterdale 'ud be a nice little spot for red squirrels. Have you seen any grey squirrels there?' he quizzed them. Mandy and James shook their heads.

'Then it's a possibility,' he said, nodding. 'Mebbe I should take a look sometime.' He turned to Ernie. 'How about you? You up for a trip out?'

'Aye, I'll come with you,' Ernie agreed. 'I want to see what Sam Western's about over there, anyhow.'

'Eh-up, young Mandy,' Walter said, looking over Mandy's shoulder. 'In't that the Animal Ark vehicle, over there by there by the green?'

Mandy shaded her eyes against the setting sun and peered over to where Walter was pointing, then stood up and waved as her dad got out of the driving seat. 'Da-ad,' she cried, 'Over here!'

Adam Hope looked round to see where the voice was coming from, then came across to the pub garden.

Walter shuffled along the bench to make space for Adam to sit down.

'Thanks, Walter, but I can't stop. I've been sent to collect these two,' he said as he reached them. 'Mum sent me out to find you,' he told Mandy. 'You'll be late for *Wildlife Ways*, and they've rescheduled the deer film, it's on tonight!' He looked at his watch. 'In half an hour, in fact. Come on, we've just got time to run James home.'

'We'd best finish up here and get home to see it then,' Walter announced, draining his glass, as Mandy and James jumped up and ran off towards the Land-rover.

They dropped James off at his house and headed back to Animal Ark.

'I wonder why the deer feature has been brought forward?' Mandy wondered aloud as they turned into the driveway.

'Don't ask me, love,' her dad said. 'I'd just walked in the door when Mum put down the phone and sent me back out so quickly my feet hardly had time to touch the floor.'

'Thanks, Dad,' Mandy said appreciatively. 'I'd have hated to miss it. I wonder if anyone else knows?'

'That,' Adam Hope said, turning off the engine, 'is a question you can ask Mum.'

Mandy jumped down and ran inside.

'I know what you're going to ask,' Emily Hope told her. 'And I've phoned everyone I could think of. I even phoned the Hunters, in case Dad didn't find you both.'

'Did Michelle say why the programme was brought forward?' Mandy asked.

'Yes, apparently the producer thought it was so topical, he didn't want to wait another week,' Emily Hope replied. Mandy followed her mum into the sitting-room and turned on the television. Her dad joined them as the familiar *Wildlife Ways* theme tune began. Mandy felt a shiver of excitement.

Michelle began to speak. 'We're here at Glisterdale Grange to film the herd of fallow deer whose ancestors roamed in the forest here hundreds of years ago,' she said, as the camera showed the Grange behind her. 'Glisterdale deer can wander freely about the estate, although they are not allowed in the spectacular gardens and care has been taken to protect the new young trees.'

'Look, there's James,' Mandy cried, pointing at the screen. James was measuring his height against the tree guards. And then there were the deer, running, jumping and frolicking, their coats glistening in the sunlight.

'Whose funny face is that?' Adam Hope joked, as the film showed Mandy talking to a workman.

'Do you mind, Dad? Mandy protested. 'That's me! And that's Steve I'm talking to. He's worked with deer in Scotland.'

'Take no notice, Mandy, you look fine,' Emily Hope smiled. They watched in silence as the film showed the fencing gradually going up. Peter Dickenson explained about the problems they were having and the deer coming out of the forest.

Then the camera focused on Michelle's face with the herd of deer running in the background. 'Deer have lived and bred happily at Glisterdale for hundreds of years,' she said sombrely. 'But who knows what the fate of the herd will be now?' The picture faded and the screen went black for several seconds. Then the closing credits and theme music started and Mandy's mum and dad turned to congratulate her.

'That was excellent, Mandy,' Mr Hope said. 'Hard-hitting and powerful. That should make people sit up and listen.'

'Very moving.' Emily Hope nodded. 'Michelle's watching the programme at

Simon's. I said you'd give her a ring afterwards.'
She turned to Mandy who was sitting in the
armchair hugging her knees. 'Are you all right,
love?'

'Mandy sniffed and nodded slowly. 'Mum,
Dad, what *do* you think will happen to the deer?'
she asked.

Mr and Mrs Hope looked at each other. Adam
Hope raised his eyebrows at his wife and she
nodded.

He clenched his hands together and took a
deep breath. 'To tell you the truth, Mandy, at
the worst they might get so distressed by the
noise and the work that they will eventually
leave,' he said sadly. Mandy's face crumpled.
'Wait, Mandy. Having said that, there is always
the possibility that they will adjust to the
upheaval and learn to live with it.'

'Deer have been known to learn to live
alongside motorways, during and after
construction,' her mum added. 'So it's not
impossible.'

'And if, between you, you can put a halt to
Sam Western's plans,' her dad said, 'well, who
knows what could happen?'

'You're right,' Mandy said, perking up.
'Thanks.' She shot her parents a grateful smile

and jumped up and went off to phone Michelle.

A few minutes later she came back into the room, smiling. 'Michelle phoned the TV station and they said that the phone hasn't stopped ringing,' she told her parents. 'They've had loads of protests about the threat to the forest and the deer.'

'There you are, then,' Mrs Hope said. 'We told you it would move people, and it has.'

'People power!' Adam Hope announced. 'Nothing like it.'

'Michelle wants to meet us at Glisterdale tomorrow to see if there are any developments,' Mandy said. 'I'll ring James now; we can meet first thing in the morning.'

Over the phone, James sounded as excited as Mandy when she told him Michelle's news. That night, as she lay in bed, Mandy felt too nervous and excited to sleep. She knew how important it was that something happened *now* to save the deer and the forest. It was good to know there were other people out there who cared too, she thought, as she eventually drifted off.

Nine

'My goodness!' Adam Hope said, staring in surprise through the windscreen of the Land-rover. Mr Hope had offered to give Mandy and James a lift to Glisterdale the next morning. But as they approached the turning to the Grange, the traffic had almost come to a standstill. Cars were queuing to enter the estate from each direction.

'Your film certainly got things moving,' Mr Hope told them. Then he checked his watch. 'The trouble is, I'll be late for my call if I wait. I think I'd better go back and cut through around the back of Law Farm.'

'OK, Dad, we can walk the rest of the way,'

Mandy said, gathering her bag and sweater.

'Thanks for the lift, Mr Hope,' said James. 'Will you be calling in later?'

'I'll see how we're fixed, James. I'd certainly like to see what's happening,' Mr Hope remarked, as he reached into the back of the Land-rover and put a sign that said 'Vet on Call' in red lettering in the windscreen. 'I expect your mother would too, Mandy,' he grinned. 'See you later.'

'Bye, Dad.' Mandy waved.

At the gates of Glisterdale, they found Bert busily directing the traffic. He was wearing an orange jacket that said 'Marshall' on the back. The main car park up ahead looked almost full already.

'Well, well, well, I'll be blowed!' Bert said as he waved another car through. 'Michelle is already here,' he told them. 'She's talking to the people that arrived last night.'

'Last *night*!' Mandy and James exclaimed together.

'Aye, last night. They're camping on the lawns,' Bert said, putting his hands on his hips. 'They've got banners and the like. Never seen nothin' like it, I haven't.'

Bert was looking a bit harassed. A group of

ramblers standing at the entrance were assembling a placard that said *Save Glisterdale Forest* and waiting to speak to him.

'Mr Dickenson left these for you,' Bert told Mandy and James, handing them sleeveless white tabards with green fluorescent stripes and 'Marshall' written on the back. 'We use 'em when we have events here. Never had nothin' like this though,' he sniffed. Mandy and James slipped them over their heads and tied them at the sides.

'We ought to go and find Michelle,' said Mandy, stepping backwards as a minibus full of excited boys from the Walton Cub group tried to squeeze its way past them.

'James, lad, can you give us a hand up here for a bit?' Bert asked him. 'It needs two of us really. I'll see 'em in, you make sure they knows where to go. We'd best open up the private car park, behind the house, too.' He plodded over to the minibus holding his hand up, palm facing forwards like a policeman directing the traffic.

'You find Michelle and I'll see you later,' James told Mandy. 'When it quietens down.'

'If it does!' Mandy answered. 'Isn't it great that so many people care enough to come here?' James nodded.

'Over here, lad!' Bert shouted from the drive and James ran to join him.

Mandy made her way over to the house, looking out for Michelle. There were little groups of people all over the grounds and along the path that led to the forest. They all seemed to be holding placards and banners protesting against the plans for the forest. At the top end of the paddock the deer huddled nervously together.

'Mandy!' a voice called. 'Over here!'

Mandy turned. Beside the house Mrs Dickenson stood talking to a young woman with short highlighted hair who wore a brown suit and was holding a briefcase. Rosie, dancing with frustration at being kept on a lead, barked as she saw Mandy approach.

'Mandy, I'm so pleased to see you,' Mrs Dickenson said smiling. 'This is Sally Hudson from the Forestry Commission.'

'Hello, Mandy,' Sally Hudson said. 'I had a long chat with Michelle last night and she told me how much you've helped in making the *Wildlife Ways* programme.'

Mandy blushed. 'My friend James helped too,' she said, stroking Rosie.

'Yes, where is James?' Sally Hudson asked.

'He's not missing this, is he?'

'He's helping Bert at the gates,' Mandy replied.

'Oh good,' Mrs Dickenson said gratefully. She glanced around anxiously at the crowd. 'Where *is* Peter? He was about to take Sally to find Michelle when we realised we're going to need some way of talking to all these people. He's gone to set up the Tannoy system. The trouble is, with all the work going on he probably can't find it!' She smiled at them both. 'Mandy, would you take Sally to meet Michelle for me, please? She said she would be interviewing the people who are camping.'

'Yes, of course, I was looking for her myself,' Mandy agreed.

Slowly they worked their way past all the people. Outside the teashop there was a line of people patiently queuing for cups of tea and coffee. Mandy paused and gazed around, then she pointed towards the forest, where groups of people were standing beside a circle of small tents.

'There she is!' she exclaimed to Sally. 'Down there by the tents.'

They hurried through the crowd, who moved aside for Mandy when they saw her marshall's vest. Michelle was busy interviewing a group of people in jeans and green sweatshirts with the logo *Forests for the Future* on them. Mandy and Sally stood to one side, listening.

'So, would you please tell our viewers what made you take this stand of camping here last night?' Michelle said to one young man. 'Just tell us in your own words.'

'Well,' the young man began, then cleared his throat and looked at Michelle.

Michelle nodded her head toward Janie and the camera, and the man turned to look at the camera.

'Well, we as a group feel very strongly that

too much forest has been lost already. There's hardly a forest left in the world that hasn't been damaged by people in one way or another.' Taking a deep breath he continued. 'As a boy I spent all my spare time in the forest watching wildlife, and I . . .' He hesitated and then, holding his arms out to indicate the others, continued, '. . . *we*, want to make sure that there are forests full of wildlife left for *our* children to walk in. We're prepared to go anywhere to stop forests being cut down simply to make money.' The young man stopped and indicated the tents. 'And we're prepared to stay until the problem is resolved.' His friends were nodding agreement.

Mandy felt a shiver of anticipation run through her. These people felt like she did. Surely between them they could save the deer.

'Thank you very much,' Michelle said, as everyone clapped. She moved across to talk to another group holding a banner that said *Save Glisterdale's Deer*. 'Would any of you like to give an opinion?' she asked.

'Yes, I certainly would,' said a woman in a smart tweed suit, stepping forward. 'The deer have been here for generations. These creatures have no means of defending themselves, or the forest they live in, from money-grabbing men who wish to steal, yes, I said *steal*, their land.' She paused for breath. 'It is up to us, the people of this country to put our foot down and say no!' she concluded.

'Hear, hear!' The group cheered so loudly they almost drowned out Michelle's response.

'Sam Western's not going to like this,' said a soft voice. Mandy turned to see James standing behind her. 'Pretty hot stuff, eh?' he said.

'You're not kidding!' Mandy whispered. Michelle was talking to the Walton Cubs now. Each of the boys held a small placard with a single letter on it. As Michelle lined them up they spelled out *Save the Deer*.

'Have people stopped arriving now?' Mandy asked James.

'There are still a few, but Bert can manage on his own now.' James told her. 'Mr Dickenson wants us up at the house.'

'Why?' Mandy asked. She was loath to leave what was fast becoming the hub of activity. 'What do you think he wants?'

'I don't know,' James replied. 'He just called out that he could use our help, as I passed the house. I said I'd go back when I found you.'

They made their way up through the crowds.

'Look, there's Gran!' Mandy cried. 'And she's brought loads of people!' She ran up to the formal gardens where Gran stood, solid and straight like a soldier, holding one end of a long banner that proclaimed *Welford Women's Institute Against Deforestation*.

'Hi, Gran,' Mandy smiled. 'I didn't know you were coming.'

'Neither did I, Mandy,' her gran replied. 'But I watched your programme last night and it made my blood boil.'

'But what about everyone else?' Mandy asked, looking down the line of banner holders. 'And what about your meeting?'

'After your mum rang last night, I called all the members and told them all about the programme,' Gran replied, 'and of course they all watched. We all feel very strongly about preserving the environment around Welford, so we put the meeting off until tomorrow.' She looked around at the mass of people. 'This is a fine turnout for a protest, Mandy, I'm sure it will do some good.'

But as Mandy walked back to the house she began to wonder what good it actually *would* do.

'I know Michelle will probably put this in the

programme next week,' she said to James, 'But
will it make any difference to Sam Western?'

'It would be better if he was actually here to
see the protest,' James admitted, 'but at least
he'll see it on the local news tonight,' he said,
looking sideways at Mandy.

Mandy spun around to face him, 'James!
Why didn't you say? How do you know?' she
exclaimed.

'There's a team from the local news
programme here filming; I let them in myself,'
James told her proudly.

'Mandy and James, just the people I need,'
Peter Dickenson called from outside the house,
where he was talking to Harry.

They ran across the drive to join him.

'And I'm telling you, sir, if you don't keep all
those people away from where we're working,
there'll be an accident,' Harry was saying to Mr
Dickenson in an angry voice. 'And I'll not be
held responsible. I've warned you now. Like it
or not, I've a job to carry out.'

'You're right,' Peter Dickenson agreed, trying
to calm him down. 'I'll make an announcement
asking people to stay on Glisterdale land.' He
turned to speak to Mandy and James. 'Would
you help me carry the sound system down to

where Michelle is,' he asked. 'Most of the people seem to be down there now. And if you could help me with this platform,' he said to Harry, 'then I'll explain to everyone that we have to stick to the law. We can't trespass on Sam Western's land. This is a proper protest, and we don't want it to get out of hand. We don't want to end up looking like a bunch of rowdy hooligans.'

Mr Dickenson lifted one side of the platform, and Harry took the other. Together they set off down the drive.

James whispered out of the corner of his mouth to Mandy, 'I couldn't ever in a million years imagine Mr Dickenson looking like a rowdy hooligan.'

'Or my gran,' Mandy added, smiling at the thought. They carried the sound system down to where the two men had set the platform down. Mr Dickenson picked up the microphone and jumped up on to the platform.

'Ladies and gentlemen,' Mr Dickenson called over the Tannoy. 'I would like to thank you all for coming here today and giving your support to Glisterdale Forest and its deer. This united stand will surely show the new owner how strong our opposition is to his plans. However,

I must ask that you keep away from where the men are working and stay on Glisterdale Grange land. Thank you.' He put down the microphone and jumped down off the platform.

'It's a shame the protesters can't take over the forest and drive the workmen out,' Mandy grumbled.

'Between you and me, Mandy, I tend to agree,' Mr Dickenson told her. 'But we have to stick to the letter of the law or Sam Western could prosecute. Life's not simple any more,' he sighed.

'Mr Dickenson, Mr Dickenson, can I have a word, please?' called a workman, pushing through the crowd towards them.

'It's Steve!' Mandy said, surprised.

Still wearing the hard hat that marked him out as one of the workmen, Steve was being booed as he passed.

'Have you got a phone I could use, in private?' he asked uneasily. 'I think Mr Western should come and see what's going on here. Some of the crowd are getting a bit stroppy. There's no way they'll let us finish the fencing, I can tell. The rest of the boys don't like what he's doing much either. Most of us agree with the demonstrators, to be honest.' He looked around to see if anyone was listening, then added, 'He's going about this the wrong way. Putting everyone's back up. It's terrible to see the deer so frightened. If I wasn't so concerned about the deer, and doing the best I can for them, I'd have walked off this job long ago.'

'You can use the phone in the office; ask my wife to show you, up at the house,' Peter Dickenson told him quickly. 'I agree, Sam Western should see this.'

Steve hurried off and Mandy and James followed Mr Dickenson down to the half-finished fence. A number of people were standing where the remainder of the fence was to go, arguing with the foreman.

'You can't do this,' a smartly dressed man in a waxed jacket was saying. 'The people are against it. You can see for yourself.' He gestured towards the rest of the crowd.

'Look, sir,' Harry said, resignedly. 'It's my job. *Our* jobs.' He indicated the rest of the men but they shook their heads and sat down on the last remaining roll of fencing. They had clearly given up. 'It's what we're getting paid to do, lads,' Harry entreated them, but they wouldn't budge. As he tried to persuade them, he was interrupted by a loud voice behind him.

'Stop this work immediately! You are breaking the law and I have proof!' Mrs Ponsonby called, pushing her way through the crowd. She was waving a large brown envelope above her head.

'Oh no,' Harry groaned, his shoulders sagging. 'It's her again.'

'In this envelope I have all the proof I need that you must leave the forest immediately,' Mrs Ponsonby declared.

Harry held out his hand. 'Let's see it, then,' he said with a huge sigh.

'Oh no you don't!' Mrs Ponsonby said, glaring at him and clutching the envelope to her chest. 'I shall only reveal this in front of the television cameras.'

'Good grief,' James whispered to Mandy. 'She'll do anything to be on telly.'

'Shh,' Mandy hissed back, stifling a giggle.

There was a long silence as everybody waited to see what would happen next. Harry stared at Mrs Ponsonby who stared back unwaveringly.

Eventually the foreman turned and walked over to the men. 'Right, lads,' he said, taking a deep breath.

'There'll be trouble if he orders them to carry on,' Mandy murmured to James.

'And he'll be in trouble if he doesn't,' James answered.

Harry turned back to face the crowd. 'From now on,' he declared, 'we're off the job until it's sorted.' A big cheer went up and Harry's red face went even redder.

'Well done, my man,' Mrs Ponsonby said, with a firm nod of her head. 'We are all behind you.'

Harry looked as if he wasn't sure whether that would be a lot of help when he had to explain himself to Sam Western.

'Might I suggest that we move right back up nearer the house,' Peter Dickenson suggested over the Tannoy. 'That will leave more room for the deer, both in the forest and on my land.'

The crowd was just moving away from the forest when a car carrying Sam Western arrived. It skidded to a halt and Dennis Saville got out, followed by Sam Western, an angry scowl on his face. As he marched through the paddocks, word went around that the new owner of Glisterdale forest had arrived. A chant went up. 'Save the forest, save the deer. Save the forest, save the deer.'

For just a few seconds, Mandy had an anxious burst of trepidation, now that a confrontation was about to happen. Then she looked around at the crowds of people, all here to support the campaign for the deer, and felt confident again.

'Get off my land!' Sam Western thundered, as he drew nearer to the forest. 'This is a work site now, not a nature reserve,' he said, turning to make sure Dennis Saville was behind him. 'A bunch of namby-pamby tree-huggers won't stop the work going ahead.' He stopped in front of Michelle and Janie. 'This is your fault, young lady,' he said, wagging a finger in Michelle's face. 'And I'm going to take it up with your employers. Misrepresentation, that's what it was. You should be ashamed of yourself!'

'Everything we said on the programme was true,' Michelle told him in a clear, firm voice, 'as all these people know.'

'All these people,' Sam Western leaned toward her, glowering, 'should have better things to do than interfere in my business.'

'We can't hear what's happening,' someone at the back of the crowd called out.

'That's just too bad,' Dennis Saville shouted back. 'Why don't you all go home?'

But quick as a flash, Mr Dickenson ran over with the microphone from the Tannoy system.

'Mr Western,' Michelle spoke into the mike.

'Let's be reasonable about this. There are lots of important facts about this forest that perhaps you weren't aware of.'

'And what might they be?' Sam Western demanded.

Mandy held her breath as she watched Michelle glance round the crowd. Then Michelle's eyes met hers and she beckoned Mandy and James over. She handed Mandy the mike and urged her forward. Mandy knew that if ever they had a chance to save the deer, it was now.

Ten

Mandy took a deep breath and spoke into the microphone. 'Well, in the war lots of soldiers did their training up here and some of the trees' – she turned and pointed – 'these beech trees near the house, are full of bullets. So they wouldn't be much good as anything but trees,' she announced in a clear voice. To her surprise, Mr Western didn't shout or bluster; he appeared to be listening.

'That's true,' a voice called out. People made way as someone pushed forward. It was Walter Pickard. 'I remember that,' he said.

'So do we,' shouted Mandy's grandad and Ernie Bell. 'Those trees would ruin any machine you put them through.'

Sam Western pulled at the lobe of his right ear and frowned.

Mandy handed the mike to James.

'Some of the oak trees,' James began, but the mike made loud popping noises. He looked desperately at Michelle who mouthed, 'Hold it further away!'

James tried again. This time it was fine. 'Some of these oak trees are more than three hundred years old,' he told the crowd. 'They have preservation orders on them and they can't be cut down. It would be against the law.'

'That's right,' a man in a waxed jacket said. 'The courts would take a very dim view of such action,' he added.

'And who might *you* be?' Sam Western said, looking perplexed.

'I am here as a conservationist today,' the man responded with a faint smile, 'but I am also a lawyer. I am perfectly happy to act for these people to see fair play is done.'

'That won't be necessary,' Sam Western assured him, looking flustered.

Peter Dickenson held a sheaf of papers in the air. 'Here's the proof, if it's needed.'

'I should like to speak now,' Mrs Ponsonby

said, moving in front of the camera.

Sam Western raised his eyebrows. Taking out a handkerchief, he mopped his brow. 'Go on, then,' he said. 'Everybody else has. You may as well put your two-pennyworth in.'

Mrs Ponsonby glared at him as she took the mike from James. She was wearing the hat with the cherries on it and they wobbled as she spoke.

'In this envelope,' she said, pausing to hold it up for everyone to see, 'is positive proof, yes, PROOF, that there are red squirrels in that forest.'

Sam Western shook his head in disbelief. 'Is that all you've got to say, woman? A bunch of squirrels!' he exclaimed.

'But,' Mrs Ponsonby said smiling a little smile of victory, 'perhaps you don't realise, *man*, that red squirrels are protected by law, and nobody, not even you, can get round that.'

'She's right,' Walter Pickard agreed. 'The law's the law, Western, you can't disturb them.'

'Let's see this proof then,' Sam Western challenged Mrs Ponsonby.

Mandy and James looked at Michelle. They'd all realised together that what was in the envelope was the photograph Mrs Ponsonby had taken the other afternoon. What would it be like? An unrecognisable dot up in the canopy? Or, even worse, would it turn out to be a grey squirrel?

Mandy held her breath as Mrs Ponsonby opened the envelope with a flourish. She held up the picture to Janie's camera.

Mandy gasped. It was a large, glossy photograph of a creature that was unmistakably a red squirrel.

'I photographed this red squirrel just a couple of days ago,' Mrs Ponsonby said, turning around so that the crowd could see the picture.

'What a perfect photograph,' Michelle said. 'May I see?' Mrs Ponsonby blushed and handed it over.

'Yes, there is no mistake,' Michelle said, passing the photograph to Peter Dickenson. 'There are red squirrels here all right. What an expert photographer you are, Mrs Ponsonby. Good enough to work on a wildlife magazine!'

'Thank you, my dear,' Mrs Ponsonby said sweetly, meeting Michelle's eyes without a waver.

'Mr Western,' Michelle said seriously, 'if all these factors aren't enough, let me try to persuade you about the benefits that could be gained from a different . . .' she paused as she searched for a tactful word, '... *attitude* to the forest. This is Sally Hudson from the Forestry Commission.' Michelle introduced Sally and handed her the mike. Sam Western looked warily at her, as if he thought she was about to arrest him.

'Mr Western, might I suggest a couple of ideas you may not have considered?' Sally began. 'After all, this has all happened rather speedily.'

'And we know why,' James muttered to Mandy.

'Before anyone could stop him, you mean,' she whispered back.

'Perhaps you had planned to fell the forest and sell off all the prime timber, Mr Western?' Sally didn't wait for an answer. 'Why not review your felling policy instead, and manage the forest in a way that would benefit everyone?'

Sam Western looked seriously at Sally. 'Go on,' he said bluntly.

Everyone listened intently as Sally explained. 'Large parts of this woodland are made up of conifers,' she pointed out. 'Why not exploit these parts and leave the deciduous woodland alone. You could fell it section by section and replant as you go along so it would be a fast-growing, renewable source of timber.'

Sam Western raised his eyebrows and looked at Sally with respect.

'If you manage it like that,' Sally continued, 'not only will you have a constant cash crop of timber, but you won't destroy this ancient forest and its wildlife. We can help you to work out a management plan for the deer. Deer can be very useful in the management of a forest. They keep the grass and shrubs under control, and as long as the herd is kept to a manageable size the forest can support them without suffering any damage.'

While Sally was speaking, Mandy gazed at the deer milling about on the edge of the crowd. One little group of five does and a fawn were standing on the drive near the house. Mandy began edging her way towards them. She looked back to see Michelle watching her. Michelle gave her a nod and Mandy made her way over to the deer. She could still hear Sally's voice through the loudspeakers.

As she reached the drive Mandy's heart leaped and a thrill of excitement rushed through her. The fawn had a neat blue ear tag! But even without it, she would have recognised Sprite. And now Mandy could see that one of the does was Honey-Mum. Slowly she moved closer. One of the does raised her tail and stamped the ground in alarm. Another gave a sharp bark. The startled group made to run away but Sprite and Honey-Mum stood their ground.

'Maaa,' Sprite called.

Mandy kneeled down and put out her hand.

Sprite wandered slowly across the drive, stretched out her neck and nuzzled into it.

'Just like you used to,' Mandy said, feeling the soft wet nose in her palm. Sprite had grown stronger in her time with the herd. Mandy could clearly see how her muscles had developed. Her eyes were bright and her glossy coat glinted in the sun.

'What's to become of you, little one?' she breathed softly. 'Your future depends on Sam Western today.'

Mandy watched in silence as Honey-Mum came nearer. And as Sprite licked her hand, she felt a hot tear slide down her cheek. These animals were so trusting, and so beautiful. She hoped desperately that Sam Western would listen to Sally Hudson. Mandy had done all she could do to save Sprite's home and she couldn't bear it if they had failed.

'And that's my suggestion for the forest, Mr Western,' Sally finished. 'I hope you'll consider it.'

Mandy stood up and watched as Sam Western took the microphone from Sally. Her legs felt like jelly and she barely noticed Sprite pulling at her shoelace.

'I've listened to everything you've said,' Sam Western's voice boomed out, 'and now it's my turn.' There was absolute silence as the crowd waited to hear his words. 'I bought this forest as a business, just like I'd buy a factory, and I admit, I'd planned to take out all the prime timber and replace it with conifers.' He waited as a murmur rippled through the crowd. 'But in the light of what I've heard today, I've decided to leave the older parts of the forest intact,' he said. 'The beeches and the oaks can all stay. I'll not touch them.'

'And the squirrels!' Mrs Ponsonby called out.

'Yes, woman. And the squirrels!' Mr Western agreed, sounding exasperated.

Everyone was cheering. Mandy hugged Sprite, then ran as fast as she could down to where Sam Western stood shaking Sally Hudson's hand.

Mandy tried to get his attention but everyone was making too much noise. 'Mr Western, please!' she shouted, so loudly that the microphone picked it up. The crowd was silent, as

Mandy stood there white-faced.

'Don't tell me you're *still* not happy, young lady?' Sam Western said, frowning.

'Mr Western, what about the deer?' Mandy asked desperately. 'You haven't said if they can stay in the forest.'

Sam Western gave a deep sigh. 'They might as well; they live there, don't they?'

'But they need to move freely and they can't,' Mandy pleaded. 'Not with the fence there.' She glanced around quickly. Mr and Mrs Dickenson were holding their breath. James had his fingers crossed, and there were her gran and grandad, looking anxious; she could almost feel them willing her on. On the edge of the crowd, Steve winked at her.

Sam Western lifted the microphone again. 'Not only have I agreed to leave the forest and,' he said, looking at Mrs Ponsonby, 'the squirrels alone, but this young lady wants me to take down the fence. The fence that I have just had put up at great cost!' he said, raising his eyebrows.

Mandy looked at her feet. She had a sudden feeling of fear that by asking this much of him, she might have made Sam Western so cross he'd change his mind about everything. She could

hardly bear to listen as he started to speak.

'I don't suppose you want deer all over your drive, do you, Dickenson?' he asked, with a chuckle. Mandy looked up in disbelief. 'All right, Harry,' Mr Western called. 'Take the fence down along this side. Just fence the parts where work is being done.'

There were whoops of joy from the crowd.

Peter Dickenson rushed over and shook Sam Western's hand. 'You won't regret this decision,' he said, gratefully.

'You're a canny man, Dickenson,' Sam Western looked at him shrewdly. 'You got what you wanted all round. I'll be needing your keeper to manage those deer, though. Saville knows nothing about them.'

'But Steve does, Mr Western,' Mandy said, grinning. 'Steve was a deer-keeper in Scotland.' She pointed Steve out in the crowd.

'Hmm, was he now?' Mr Western rubbed his chin. 'I'll have to think on that.'

Ernie Bell and Walter Pickard came over to join them.

'It's a strong man who knows when to change his mind,' Walter said to Mr Western, who looked rather pleased. But before he could reply, a group of estate workers hoisted him up on their shoulders and carried him forward to where Janie was filming. For a moment Sam Western looked flustered, but soon he was beaming at the camera.

'And so, viewers,' Michelle said, 'this is a better ending than we could possibly have imagined. The ancient forest is saved, the deer can run free again, and up above our heads, a colony of red squirrels are safe once more.'

She switched off the mike and turned to Mrs Ponsonby who was still hovering near the camera. 'Even if they haven't got their winter ear tufts like the one in your picture,' she said with a wry smile.

'I'll tell you a little secret,' Mrs Ponsonby said, beckoning Michelle, Mandy and James closer. 'When I got to Walton, I had an attack of nerves. Supposing my photograph didn't come out? All might have been lost!' she told them. 'So I popped into the library on the way and photographed one on a poster that I'd seen,' she confessed. 'It came out so much better than my other photograph, that I decided to use it instead.'

'Mrs Ponsonby, that was very naughty of you,' Michelle said, suppressing a smile.

'I have nothing to feel guilty about,' Mrs

Ponsonby declared. 'I know what I saw, dear, and one red squirrel is very like another.'

What with Mrs Ponsonby's trick and Mr Western's performance as the hero of the day, Mandy and James were giggling so much, they could hardly stand up.

'Well done, love,' said a voice behind them. Adam Hope put an arm around Mandy's shoulder.

'We arrived just as you started speaking,' Emily Hope told her. 'We heard it all.'

Peter Dickenson came over to the group. 'We've been hugely successful today, Mandy,' he said. 'And everyone knows that saving the deer was down to your persistence. Sam Western thinks that he's going to put Steve in charge of the herd, and he's asked if I will help out with some advice.'

'So Sprite and Honey-Mum are safe now,' Mandy said, feeling a warm glow of success spread through her.

'As safe as they'll ever be,' Michelle said, as she joined them. 'Imagine, we came to film a deer herd and ended up saving a forest. Just think how impressed the viewers will be when we show the footage on next week's programme. This will be a hard act to follow!'

While Michelle spoke to Peter Dickenson and Mr and Mrs Hope, Mandy and James walked back down to the forest. Although most of the people had started to leave now, the campers were still packing up their tents.

'Look,' James said, pointing at the groups of deer that were leaving the paddocks and returning to the forest. 'They're going home!'

'Good,' Mandy declared happily. 'It's where they belong.'